CRIME SCENE

FROM THE INSIDE OUT!

Gene Thatcher

Order this book online at www.trafford.com
or email orders@trafford.com

Most Trafford titles are also available at major online book retailers.

Printed in the United States of America.

ISBN: 978-1-4669-8897-2 (sc)
ISBN: 978-1-4669-8899-6 (hc)
ISBN: 978-1-4669-8898-9 (e)

Library of Congress Control Number: 2013906103

Trafford rev. 09/11/2013

Trafford PUBLISHING® www.trafford.com

North America & international
toll-free: 1 888 232 4444 (USA & Canada)
fax: 812 355 4082

CONTENTS

INTRODUCTION

OVERVIEW

It's 1:30 in the morning and Mr. Williams is awakened by the doorbell ringing. He goes downstairs and opens the door. Two men in suits with badges are standing there. The street is full of police and emergency vehicles. People are shuffling back and forth. Across the street he sees yellow barrier tape that says "CRIME SCENE—KEEP OUT". A Crime Scene van is parked in front of the house across the street and he sees the Medical Examiner arrive. What is going on?

Thousands of crimes happen in the United States every day. Some are violent crimes with the most serious outcome and others are not so serious yet still traumatize its victims. Many of these crimes require a crime scene unit to process them in order for these crimes to be solved.

Crime Scene—It sounds like a violent place. What exactly does it mean? How big is it? What's in it? Who's in it? Is it dangerous? Should I take my family away? Why can't they give us any information? I'm confused, worried and scared. Why do they need so many people? Can anyone give us any answers?

<u>Processed</u>—What does that mean and what does it entail? Who are these people doing the processing and what's going on in there? What's in all those cases they are carrying in? Why are they dressed like that? Why are there so many of them? Am I safe? Nobody is telling us anything, why?

I will try to answer all these questions. We'll go from what constitutes a crime scene and what we do there to examining a selection of cases and the different problems they present. A broad statement would be to say that every crime scene is examined and processed in the same way. This is an accurate assumption but you must keep an open mind. Different crimes scenes present a different set of questions which must be answered. At the end of each of these cases I will address these items. I will also address some of the words and terminology used as well as what a crime lab is and what they do there.

DEDICATION

This book would not be made possible without the backing of my wife Janet and my family. I can't even count the birthdays, holidays, dinners and many family functions they have endured without me. Their understanding and support was unheralded. It seemed like every time an event was scheduled something would happen where I would not be able to attend or would have to leave prior to its conclusion.

In addition this book is for all those crime scene and law enforcement people who dedicate their lives to finding the truth. There is no such thing as a clock or schedule on their lives. They work as needed 24 hours a day 7 days a week. They endue great sacrifice to family. They are deprived of sleep, hot food and work in all types of weather. They don't get extra pay or rewards for what they do only the satisfaction of knowing what they do is a necessity. They work in some of the most difficult of atmospheres and conditions. They deal with death, biological hazards and distressed citizens daily. Every time a crime is committed they respond without question. They see on a daily basis some of the most terrible events that can happen to us. They see the pain and suffering and have the fortitude to continue on in situations most of us could never imagine. They must be professional at all times keeping their feelings inside. A noted forensic expert once wrote in the front cover of his book I purchased "Thank you for your work". That says it all. They make a difference and ask for nothing in return.

ABOUT THE AUTHOR

Born in Brooklyn, New York and raised and educated in New Jersey, Gene Thatcher worked in several different fields before settling down in Law Enforcement in 1984. He is a Navy veteran of the Viet Nam War. He started working as a corrections officer before going to the Sheriff's office. After a short tour in the county courts he was transferred to the Crime Scene Division where he stayed nearly 22 years until his retirement in 2010. During that length of time he processed crime scenes and collected evidence from those scenes. The last 8 years he worked primarily as a latent fingerprint examiner. He was the supervisor of the latent print examination section and crime scene supervisor up and until his retirement.

Gene attended many crime scene schools throughout our nation. Not only was he a well-schooled student of his field but he shared his knowledge and training by becoming a Certified Police Instructor by the New Jersey Police Training Commission. He has taught police recruits in the training academies as well as seasoned officers from around the United States and foreign countries for over 19 years. He has instructed training classes for Federal Bureau of Investigation as well as other federal agencies, The International Association of Identification (IAI) and many others. He is a member of the International Association of Identification—New Jersey

Division, the International Association of Arson Investigator and the New Jersey Homicide Investigator Association. He has also been honored by many police agencies.

CHAPTER ONE

The Crime Scene

The best place to start is by defining what a crime scene is. A crime scene is simply any place a crime has occurred. It could be as small as a square foot or less, or it can be large covering several places in different areas or even different states. Most of the time, the crime scene is easily seen or defined. It is physical things that can be seen by the naked eye or items that have been disturbed or broken. It can be that things are physically not seen mainly because they are very small or missing. Then there are the things that are there but can't be seen. Things such as fingerprints, DNA, hairs, fibers and chemical residues. These items may require forensic processing. At times they can be processed at the scene. Some require processing at the crime lab or other locations. Crime scenes can be inside or outside of buildings. It can be a vehicle or just a single item. Every crime scene varies and is different. As different and varied as they are they are all for the most part are processed in the same manner. Some require more processing then others. Processes differ from item to item but the end result is always to achieve the same result, the truth of what happened. Crime scene investigators follow a procedure that is the same for all scenes. Some of the steps may be eliminated from some scenes while some may be added to others depending on the items to be processed and the circumstances surrounding the scene. A quick example would be why process for DNA if there are no body fluids present? Why call the Medical Examiner if there isn't a body present?

Let's examine a couple of typical crime scenes. I'll use the word typical but there is no such thing as a typical crime scene. A better word would be a basic crime scene. We'll assume that you are our victim. You pull into the driveway after a long day of shopping and as you do you notice that your trash can has been moved and is under your kitchen window. The window is pushed up. You get out of your car and go to the front door and see that it is slightly open. You push the door open and look inside only to see that your entire house is ransacked. You enter and see that cabinets and drawers are opened. Your TV set and stereo equipment is gone. During further examination of your home you find that other items are gone. Your wife's jewelry is gone and so are your child's video games. You've been burglarized! You call the police. A patrolman arrives and takes a report. You answer dozens of questions. The officer then tells you that he is notifying the crime scene unit. He requests that you do not enter the residence until the crime scene unit arrives. It takes a while but the crime scene unit arrives. The detective identifies himself and again asks you several questions. These question are more on the line of what's missing, the time you were gone and other question like "did you touch anything when you entered?"

The detective then begins his examination of the scene. He starts where the actor started, the kitchen window.

The first thing he does is take photographs of the entire scene starting at the kitchen window and going through the house in the same order that the actor did. He takes overall photographs of the scene as well as detailed photographs of the areas that were disturbed and of items the he determines to be of value from an evidence stand point. These are the items that he will process or collect to take to the crime lab for processing. Sometimes if the scene is large or extensive he may take a video recording of the scene. The photographing and video recordings of the scene are necessary to preserve a visual record of the scene. This and all the rest of what he does may someday have to go to court and be presented to a jury. Documentation is very important when it comes to trials and juries. Once the photographing and video recording is completed the detective will start to process the scene for evidence. If the scene is large or difficult he may request addition detectives to assist him. He will decide at this point which items he can process on scene and which items need to be taken back to the crime lab to be processed. When he finishes he will determine what he will collect and bag the evidence that has to be taken to the crime lab. He will then process the remaining items at the scene. He will probably start dusting for latent fingerprints at the point of entry, the kitchen window. Before we continue let me explain the term latent fingerprints. The word latent means that what you are looking for is not visible to the naked eye and has to be developed to be seen. This is usually done with powders but there are other things that can be used as well such as chemicals, lighting angles while photographing and even using lasers. If he develops a fingerprint he will collect it. This may be accomplished by using lifting tape and placing the tape on a card to preserve it. It may be that the surface that the fingerprint is on is not suitable for the use of lifting tape. In this case he may have to photograph the fingerprint using various lighting methods. One of these lighting methods could be by the use of a laser or an alternate light source. Actually lasers are not used that often anymore. A laser is basically a very bright light that operates in a specific light band and are very expensive. Alternate light sources are bright lights that use different colors to get to different light bands. It is much cheaper to buy and operate an alternate light source, while a laser only operates in one light range. The alternate light source operates in several different light bands. These light bands for the most part work best with florescent powders. In laboratory processing these light sources are combined with superglue processing and dye staining to further enhance the development.

The detective will continue to process for latent fingerprints throughout the scene. The items he processes are done one at a time until he reaches the exit area, in this case the front door. In addition to the interior or the residence the detective will also examine the exterior or the building. He will be looking for things of evidence outside the scene. Remember our trash can under the kitchen window? He would want to process the trash can as well. He would also look around the can on the ground for possible footwear impressions. These would have to be photographed as well and he might even take a casting of the footwear impression. Other areas of interest would be the way the actor entered or exited the property. These areas would also need to be photographed. When a large amount or large items are taken it may be hard to take them away all at once and they may be hidden outside or somewhere close by. For this reason a search of the area may be needed.

When the detective completes his examination he will place the evidence he has collected in his vehicle to be returned to the crime lab. He will advise you of the items he has taken and explain that they will be returned to you when the crime lab is done with them. There may be some items, depending on the circumstances, that may take a while to return to you. He will advise you that his report will be sent to the detective assigned to investigate the case. If he has developed any fingerprints in your home he will also take the fingerprints of all the residents so as to be able to eliminate their fingerprints from his findings. After all you live there, your fingerprints are supposed to be there. By this time the detective assigned to investigating the case may or may not have contacted you. If he hasn't he will and again you will be asked more questions. In a perfect situation where the actor is caught you will be notified. If the case goes to court you may or may not have to testify at the trial in which case a prosecuting attorney will contact you.

That is generally what happens in a basic crime scene. Now let's make things a bit different. You walk outside to get your mail and notice a police car next door. Just about the same time three more police cars arrive with lights flashing and sirens blaring. You see a police officer putting up yellow barrier tape that says "CRIME SCENE—DO NOT CROSS". An officer approaches you and asks you if you have been home all day? You say yes and ask him what's happened. He says that there has been an incident next door but won't say what. He asked if you saw anything or anyone around the area in the last day or so. You say no, you come to find out later that a homicide has occurred next door. There are police all over and the Crime Scene unit arrives. The detective talks to several officers and is taking notes as he speaks to them. Shortly thereafter several more Crime Scene units arrive and now there are several detectives on the scene. They are all involved in conversations and taking notes. They seem to separate and go to their vehicles. They all start heading in the direction of the house next door. They meet and talk. One of them places a large paper mat at the entrance to the house and then they both put on paper shoe covers, coveralls and latex gloves. They enter the house with the first police officer you saw when you went out to get the mail. He also puts on the shoe covers, coveralls and gloves. They spend several minutes in the house. When they exit they take off the paper shoe covers and rubber gloves and place them in a two large paper bags. The patrolman returns to his patrol car and starts writing. The detective meets with the other detectives. At this point another detective puts on paper shoe covers, coveralls and rubber gloves and takes a video camera and a still camera into the house with him. The others wait outside with cases of equipment. Two of the detectives seem to be examining the exterior of the house. They then take a video camera and a still camera and start to video and photograph the exterior of the house. A third detective is walking with them placing colored flags on the ground in areas that are pointed out by the other two detectives. After about forty minutes the detective that entered the house comes out and again places his paper shoe covers and gloves in the large paper bags. All the detectives then meet again and seem to be discussing something. Two more detectives approach the house. They seem to be carrying what looks like a small canister type vacuum cleaner. They also put on paper shoe covers and rubber gloves. You then hear the vacuum start up. Well a lot has happened up to this point but what?

Let's go back to the beginning, the officer you saw out front when you went to get the mail is what's known as the first responder. He was called to the scene when the postal carrier noticed that the mail hadn't been taken out of the mail box for three days. The officer responded to make a health and welfare check. He found that the door was unlocked, entered and found the resident dead on the floor with what appeared to be several gunshot wounds to the head and chest. He checked to house to see if there were any more victims or if the actors were still in the house. He also observed that the house was in disarray as if someone was searching for something. He left the house careful not to touch anything and called headquarters notifying them of the situation. Headquarters then sent the crime scene unit to his location. When the first unit arrived the detective talked to the first responding officer getting details of what he saw, the condition of the scene when he entered and what he did inside. When the other crime scene units arrived the first detective relayed to the other detectives the information he received from the first responding officer. They then decided who would do what aspects of the scene examination. The first detective on scene then went into the scene with the first responding officer to trace his steps as he went through the house. They put on shoe covers, coveralls and gloves so as to not contaminate the crime scene with foreign substances from outside the scene. They also saved the shoe covers, coveralls and gloves to keep any trace evidence that they may have picked up inside the scene. A detective entered the house with a video camera and still camera to document the scene as how it actually existed at the time of the detective's arrival. Again the shoe covers, coveralls and gloves were worn and saved to prevent cross contamination. This detective has to be very precise in his documentation of the scene with video and still photographs. Down the road as the investigation continues questions may arise as to specific items which may help in the prosecution of the case. An actor or suspect may have left or moved something that can tie him to the case and the video or stills can substantiate these facts. The three detectives outside are looking for items of evidence outside pertaining to the crime. This could be footwear impressions, cigarette butts, candy wrappers, tire impression, etc. The entire exterior of the house is also documented to see if there are any signs of forced entry. The officer with the flags is marking items that are found or those things that appear to be relevant to the crime scene. When these tasks are completed the detectives will meet and relay to each other their findings and completed tasks. The two officers who enter the building with the vacuum cleaner are there to vacuum but not the way you think. Their purpose is to collect trace evidence. Trace evidence is smaller items of evidence such as hairs and fibers. Part of the reason for the shoe covers and gloves is to keep trace from outside from going into the scene and trace from inside going outside. This is known as the Locard's Principle. The principle was developed by Edmond Locard, a French forensic scientist. He was said to be the Sherlock Holmes of France. His principle is known as "Every contact leaves a trace." Locard's Principle simply put is when you enter one area from another area you bring something from the area you came from into the area you are going into. For the same reason when you are in a crime scene, you take evidence away from the crime scene to the area you are going to. The detectives with the vacuum will vacuum all the areas in the crime scene including the victim's body. A different canister is used for each area. Each canister is appropriately marked. When the detectives are done with the vacuuming process detectives can enter the crime scene without shoe covers. Detectives will wear rubber gloves at all times while in the crime scene from start to finish so as not to leave fingerprints behind or damage fingerprints which are already there that haven't as yet been developed.

Now the scene has been cleaned so the team can enter the house. Once inside a multitude of things are starting to happen. First is a scanning type search of each area is made. This is a preliminary search to locate obvious pieces of evidence. These items are noted. Also at this point the Medical Examiner is notified to examine the body. Upon his arrival he will examine the body for wounds and trauma aside from the obvious ones noted during the initial response. In most cases he will give a time of death or try to establish one as close as he can. A lot of factors can help determine the time of death. Some of these items can be body temperature, room temperature, lividity, rigor mortis and decomposition. In most cases when the Medical Examiner is done the body is removed from the scene and taken to the morgue to await autopsy. The Medical Examiner will decide when the autopsy will be done.

The body is then made ready for transport to the morgue. That means that the hands must be bagged to preserve any trace evidence which may be present specifically under the finger nails. The body is placed on a clean shroud (sheet) and then placed in a clean body bag. The body bag is marked with the name, date of birth, time of death of the deceased and the name of the physician who pronounce the victim dead. The bag is then sealed by a detective who also signs and dates the seal. He also photographs the bag and seals. The victim's body can then be removed to the morgue.

The scene can then be processed much the same as it was in our burglary scene before. There are a significant number of other processes which have to be done in addition to what we did before. First of all blood samples may be collected. You ask why, we have a victim who's shot, so the blood is obviously his right? Wrong, suppose our actor cut himself or was injured when he fired the gun? The samples can place someone else in the scene. We also must look for spent shell casings from the gun. There may be projectiles which passed through the body and struck the walls or floor. If so the projectiles must be recovered for later ballistics test should we find a firearm at the scene or find one at a later time during the investigation. The possibility also exists that our victim may not have been shot where his body was found. The entire house needs an in depth search. Was the gun our victim's? Was it taken from him during a struggle? Did the actor bring it with him? These are only some of the questions that need to be answered. Other things must be noted. Was the TV on, is there food on the table or on the stove. This is crucial if food is found in the victim's stomach at the autopsy. Is it the same? This could help establish a more accurate time of death. In addition to all the photographs and video taken a sketch of scene must also be made. On that sketch all the evidence that was collected, the victim's body, blood stains, shell casings or anything important to the case must be measured in. This is useful at time of trial to illustrate to the jury the position of these items within the scene as sometimes photographs do not show these things in their proper prospective. A reason for the crime may be able to be determined. Was it robbery, drug related, a domestic? These are things that may also be found out at the crime scene.

When the scene processing and examination is complete the crime scene unit leaves the scene and in most cases all doors and windows are sealed and an officer is posted outside pending the outcome of the autopsy. This is done in the event that during the autopsy additional evidence is needed. The crime scene unit can return to the scene. The reason being, that once the crime scene is released the investigators cannot reenter the scene without a court order.

The autopsy is actually another crime scene. The autopsy is performed by a pathologist and is done to determine the cause and manner of death. That sounds like it could be confusing. Let's take a look at this. We know our victim was shot. Did one of the gunshot wounds actually kill the victim? If so our cause of death is a gunshot wound or multiple gunshot wounds. If not what did kill our victim, strangulation, poison? This is why we autopsy. The cause of death is what actually caused our victim's death. The manner of death also has questions. Was our victim murdered? Was it suicide? Was it an accident? The manner of death, the reason our victim died weather by the hand of someone else or by his own hand. Some of the things looked for are gunshot residue. The small particles of unburned gun powder left on skin or clothing. Toxicology is made to see if poisons were ingested. All body organs are examined for diseases. The throat is checked for strangulation. Other signs of trauma are looked for. The body is checked for defense wounds. This could be crucial at time of trial. Are there signs of sexual assault? This again would be crucial at time of trial. I mentioned it before but let's not forget about all the fingerprint processing and evidence collection. The difference here is that usually homicide evidence is held much longer and may never be returned. As I stated earlier there could be more than one location for the crime scene. Was our victim killed here or somewhere else and then brought here? Was our actor captured in another state with the murder weapon and proceeds from the crime?

This crime scene contained much more than the burglary discussed before. Another difference is the burglary may take a few hours to process where a homicide investigation can take days. Other crimes take more or less time to process such as auto theft, sexual assault, kidnapping etc.

CHAPTER TWO

Evidence and Processing

Evidence—Let's start with evidence. You heard it being made reference to and hear about it being collected and processed. What are they talking about? Before we can collect it or process it we need to know what it is. Evidence by definition is: Anything that tends to prove or disprove the facts at hand. Simply it is items or knowledge that helps prove or not prove what happened. That sounds pretty simple but there are different types of evidence. I'm not referring to say a bottle as compared to a bullet but more like "real" "direct" or "circumstantial". There are some big differences here. By differences I mean not only what they are but also their creditability and how they are viewed in an investigative or court atmosphere. I'll break them down one at a time and show how they differ.

Real Evidence—Just by the sound of it you can pretty much figure out what it is. Real as in the actual object, say the actor left something behind like a screw driver. Maybe he touched a water glass and left a fingerprint on it. Real objects such as a weapon like a gun, knife, and baseball bat or footwear impression. These are physical items that leave very little to question as to what it is. A gun is a gun. A water glass is a water glass. These items are not open to question as to what they are. When this type of evidence is presented in court they make it unquestionable as to what it is. Everybody knows and sees it. This is your best form or evidence. It is what it is. These items are usually easy to collect unless size or location presents a collection problem.

Direct Evidence—This presents a different set of circumstances. Direct evidence is best described as an eyewitness account. With direct evidence there isn't a physical object to actually see but a personal account of what was seen or heard. In this area another situation can come into play, such as credibility. Is the witness credible? There is a lot to take into account here. Most of the time, the witness is an upstanding citizen of the community or not. Let us say that you are at the bank waiting in line when a man comes in wearing a ski mask. He has a gun and approaches the counter window. He hands the teller a note and a bag. The teller takes money from the drawer, puts it in the bag and hands it back to the man. The man turns towards you and the other people in line, waves the gun at you and quickly leaves the bank. The teller tells everyone don't move or touch anything. The doors are locked and the police are called. When the police arrive they interview everyone in the bank. Everybody gives the police a description of the man and what they saw. For the most part everyone's story and description is about the same. This adds to everyone's credibility. This doesn't mean case closed by any means. You may have said the man had a black ski mask and black revolver. The person behind you may have said that the ski mask was navy blue and the gun was a black semi-automatic pistol. The stories are close but slightly different. When I taught recruit classes in the police academy

I would take the first recruit in the classroom and tell him a story away from the rest of the class. I would then have that recruit take the next recruit out of the classroom and relate the story to the next recruit. That recruit would repeat the process to the next recruit. This process would repeat itself until the 40 to 60 recruits all heard the story. I would then ask the last recruit to tell the story to the class that he had just heard. I would also have the first recruit relate the story as I had told it to him. The result was that the first and last stories somewhat resembled each other. Most of the time there were major differences in the stories. This proves that although direct evidence is one of you best forms of evidence it is open to question.

In the scenario above we are assuming that all the people in the bank line are perfect citizens. We don't know if they are or not but under the circumstances we can assume they are and there are no reasons to question their creditability. What if we are called to an assault at a crack house? The story that we are told is that a man was minding his own business smoking a crack pipe. Two masked males enter the crack house and beat the man with baseball bats, then fled. There are five witnesses to the assault. They all give you statements as to how the events of the beating occurred. Although all the stories sound basically similar there are many differences. The account of what happened are similar but the description of the actors and weapons vary quite a bit. You know that somewhere in this collection of statements is an accurate account of what happened. Again we ask which of these witnesses are credible. Not as simple as real evidence. These are the things that cause jury's nightmares. One of the ways we try to avoid some of these problems is to make sure that we always keep the witnesses separated from each other. Think about it, you thought that you saw a black ski mask and someone else said that it was navy blue. You hear this and start to second guess yourself. Was it black or was it navy blue? You've also heard the expression **"hear say"**. This is part of direct evidence in that it is second hand. All the courts that I have been in will not allow **"hear say"** evidence. Another words **you** heard **him** say that **"she had a gun."** As true as the statement may or may not be it's not credible. There is no way to confirm if it is true or not. You can't say for certain that you saw her with a gun. Another expression that we hear that relates to this is **"it's your word against theirs."** Both of you say opposite things. Who's right or telling the truth?

This brings us to the most difficult types of evidence, Circumstantial Evidence. What does that mean and is it good or bad? Let's start by defining what circumstantial evidence is. Circumstantial evidence tends to prove the facts at hand by inference. That means that the circumstances surrounding the investigation can be related to the investigation by association. Seems to be getting pretty complicated right here. Are we on the verge of "hear say?" To better explain this I can use a basic example of what we are talking about. Here's our first scenario. We will start out by using direct evidence. You are an eyewitness. You are standing on the street in front of an apartment building. It's daytime. You observe a green convertible pull up in front of the building. A man gets out, you recognize him, its Bob Swayer. He's wearing brown pants and shoes. He also is wearing a white pullover shirt and black ball cap. Swayer enters the building and goes to the front apartment on the first floor. He enters the apartment and is talking to another man. You see both of them in the open window. The man who lives in the apartment is wearing a dark blue bathrobe. Their conversation gets loud and they start arguing about a female. The man in the bathrobe pushes Sawyer and tells him to "get out". Swayer reaches under his shirt, pulls out a silver gun from his waistband, points it at the man in the bathrobe and shoots him two times. The man in the bathrobe falls to the floor. Swayer runs out of the building, gets into the convertible and speeds off. You see the license plate and write down the number. The police are called, you tell them what happened. They check the license plate number and confirm that the car belongs to Bob Swayer. We can agree here that this is direct evidence as seen by you, in detail, the eyewitness. You can identify the shooter. There are no other witnesses around so we assume you are a good witness and credible.

Now let's revisit our scenario. Again you are an eyewitness. You are standing on the same street in front of the same building. It's night time and dark. The street light nearest you is out. You observe a dark convertible pull up in front of the building. A man gets out. He looks a little like Bob Swayer. He's wearing dark pants and dark shoes. He's also wearing a white shirt and a dark hat. The man enters the building and goes to the front apartment on the first floor. He starts talking to another man. You hear them because the window is open but you can't see them because the room isn't lit. You only see shadows. The conversation gets loud. You hear someone say "get out". Then you hear two loud bangs and see two quick flashes. A man runs out of the building, gets into the car and speeds off. You see the license plate and write down the number. The police are called you tell them what happened. They check the license plate number and confirm the car belongs to Bob Sawyer. We agree here that in fact a man has been shot. You are an eyewitness. Can you identify the actor? There are no other witnesses around.

In our first scenario it was daytime, you saw the crime and could identify the actor. Case closed, this is direct evidence. In our second scenario it was night time. You heard a crime happen. You think you know who the actor was. There is evidence of a crime. There is a vehicle belonging to Bob Sawyer. You think it was Bob Sawyer, but is it? Was it somebody who looks like Bob Sawyer? Did he borrow Bob Sawyer's car? Now it's time for the police to build a case. Where was Bob Sawyer at the time of the crime? Where was his car? Does he have an alibi? We can infer that Bob Sawyer is in fact our actor but we need more evidence. The evidence we have is circumstantial. If we have enough circumstantial evidence and strong circumstantial evidence we may have a case. I will discuss cases where circumstantial evidence was enough to get a conviction a little later on.

Processing—Processing is exactly what it says, processing. The processing is as varied as the evidence itself. Different processes are used when looking for specific things. That is to say that looking for fingerprints is a different process than looking for DNA. Both are different procedures but both are trying to reach the same result—the truth. Our most basic process is documentation. This could be written, photographs, videos etc. From there I would say that the most common process is fingerprinting. Fingerprinting is what we do to uncover fingerprints from items which are not visible to the eye. Most of the time fingerprint development is done with dusting powders. Powders work best on non-porous surfaces. Powders come in a variety of colors to contrast the variety of surfaces. Basically you don't want to use black powder on a black car. You would best be served by using gray, silver or white. By the same token you wouldn't use red powder on a red can when black would work better. Once you develop the fingerprint you must collect it to preserve it. How do we do that? Again in most cases cellophane tape works best. The tape is carefully placed over the developed fingerprint, rubbed gently and carefully lifted up. It can then be placed on a card, again to contrast the color, and saved. It must be recorded as to where it was collected, and by whom. As with all collected evidence documentation is very important. It must be marked with place of collection, date, time, collector, case number and if possible a sketch of where it was lifted. It must also be assigned an evidence number and the card should be photographed. It must then be protected and stored in an evidence locker. There are times when powders will not work because of the surface such as something that is porous. In this case a chemical may be required to develop the fingerprint. This produces a fingerprint which is difficult to lift. To document this fingerprint it must be photographed. Then the same procedures are followed as that of a lifted print. Another method that is used quite often is what they call fuming. Fuming is a process where cyanoacrylate is used. That process is also known as super gluing. To achieve this, the piece of evidence in question is placed in a chamber. The super glue is placed in the chamber then the chamber has humidity pumped in. The fumes of super glue mixed with the humidity adhere to the fingerprints. The fingerprints show a white substance which has covered the fingerprints. The fingerprints are then dyed stained. The fingerprints are then made subject to laser light which makes the dye on the fingerprints fluoresce. They can then be photographed and documented as we did before.

We should discuss fingerprints for a moment to help you understand some things about fingerprints. First of all fingerprints are a part of us all of our lives. The truth is that fingerprints are formed on the fetus in the womb in the tenth week of pregnancy. They are the small lines on our fingers hands and feet. They stay with us our entire lives and actually are one of last thing to decompose on our bodies after death. Fingerprints outlive us. Fingerprints are composed of 98.5% to 99.5% water. The remaining .5% to 1.5% is lipids, fats and amino acids. It is these items that are left behind when we touch something. The water for the most part evaporates. Fingerprints can last seconds or years or any time in between. They are fragile to touch and atmospheric conditions. One other fact I would like to touch on is that fingerprints are unique to all of us. No two are the same. Just as all leaves, tree limbs and snowflakes are all different. No two fingerprints have ever been found alike.

Other processing procedures are collection of biological fluids for DNA analysis. DNA is the genes stored in our body cells and with the exception of identical twins are just as distinguishable as fingerprints. In the last number of years data bases are being compiled using DNA just as we have built enormous data bases of fingerprints.

Through the use of forensic laboratories we have developed sciences to compare hair, fibers and wood. We use microscopes to compare ballistics and elaborate scientific equipment such as GC Mass spectrometers to test drugs and fluids. The use of GPS equipment and computers aid us in accident investigation and crime scene sketches. The modern forensic investigator has to be more than an officer. He has to be scientist, computer specialist and investigator all rolled into one. He also has to be a law enforcement office to protect the public. As we all know television is jammed with police and forensic shows. I must state at this time however most of what you see on television is true. Some is not. There are times I wish I had some of the equipment they use but the fact remains that it just hasn't been invented yet.

I could write another book on evidence and processing. I just tried to give you some insight as to how the forensic world really works behind the closed doors. Most of the time it's a lot of hard work to maybe recover that one tiny piece of evidence that solves the crime.

Words and Terms

<u>Alibi</u>—a judicial mode of defense under which a defendant proves or attempts to prove that he/she was in another place when a crime was committed.

<u>ALS</u>—also known as an Alternate Light Source is a light which produces different light beams in different wave lengths.

<u>Amino Acid</u>—An organic compound containing an amino group (NH 2).

<u>Autopsy</u>—also known as a post-mortem examination.

Blood Splatter—The science of bloodstain pattern analysis as it applies to scientific knowledge from other fields to solve practical problems at crime scenes.

Chemilumiesence—a light producing chemical reaction similar to the same process which makes fire flies glow.

Circumstantial Evidence—Information or items that tend to prove the matter or facts at hand by inference.

Crime Lab—A scientific laboratory using primarily forensic science for the purpose of examining evidence from crime scenes.

Cyanoacrylate—More commonly known as super glue. Used for fuming evidence in the development of fingerprints.

Direct Evidence—An eyewitness account of events from personal knowledge.

DNA—Deoxyribonucleic acid is a nucleic acid that contains the genetic instructions used in the development and functioning of all known living organisms.

Dye Staining—A process by which a mixture of a Vitamin B compound is dissolved in methanol, than used to rinse items that have been developed with super glue.

Evidence—Anything that tends to prove or disprove the facts at hand.

Fingerprints—The friction ridges on the finger surfaces that form patterns and are used for identification of individuals.

Footwear Impressions—Pattern marks left behind, in or on surfaces of shoes, boots etc.

Forensics—The application of a broad spectrum of sciences to answer question of interest to the legal system.

Fuming—The process by which super glue is introduced into a humidity chamber to have it adhere to latent fingerprints left on objects.

GPS—Also known as Global Positioning System. A satellite based worldwide locating system.

Hear Say—A part of direct evidence in that it is second hand.

Hemoglobin's—Hemoglobin's are oxygen carrying proteins in the blood.

IAI—International Association of Investigation An international organization of forensic identification investigators and scientist.

IAAI—International Association of Arson Investigators An international organization of arson investigators and scientist.

Laser—A bright light source produced by speeding up a light beam to increase its intensity. Also has industrial uses.

Latents—Refers to fingerprints that are not visible to the eye but have to be developed by methods as dusting or fuming.

Lipids—A broad group of naturally occurring molecules which includes fats, waxes, sterols, fat-soluble vitamins.

Luminol—A chemical solution that reacts with hemoglobin's. Primarily used to locate blood and biologic fluids not visible to the eye.

Mass Spectrometer—An analytical technique that measures the mass-to-charge ratio of charged particles. It is used for determining masses of particles, for determining the elemental composition of a sample or molecule, and for elucidating the chemical structures of molecules, such as peptides and other chemical compounds.

Medical Examiner—A medically qualified officer whose duty is to investigate deaths and injuries that occur unusual or suspicious circumstances, to perform post-mortem examinations and in some jurisdictions initiate inquest.

Mummification—A process where the body dries out and adheres to the bone rather than go through the process of decomposition.

Non-Porous—Surfaces that do not absorb moisture or liquids.

Porous—Surfaces that do absorb moisture or liquids.

Processing—Tests, procedures and documentation used on evidence to produce desired results.

Real Evidence—A physical object as opposed to witness statements and assumptions.

Search Warrant—A legal paper granting the searching for and collection of evidence that must be sworn to and signed by a Judge or Magistrate.

Super Glue—A fast drying glue made of 100% ethyl cyanoacrylate.

Toxicology—A branch of biology, chemistry, and medicine concerned with the study of the adverse effect of chemicals on living organisms. It is the study of symptoms, mechanisms, treatments and detection of poisoning, especially the poisoning of people.

Trace Evidence—Evidence that occurs when different objects contact one another. Such material are often transferred by heat induced by contact friction.

CHAPTER THREE

You Can Do It and We Can Help

Over the years I have investigated many, many crimes. It never ceases to amaze me why and how some of these crimes are committed. I have tried to name this and the following chapters to reflect those crimes and the possible reasons they were committed. Some of these will be sad, some humorous and some just plain cold blooded.

Just by the title of this chapter you can see where this is headed. As easy as it may sound the act of suicide is not something that you just do. Most of the time there is another underlying set of circumstances or events that drive people to do this. Before we continue I would like to say that suicide is not a crime but a tragic act. Think about it you can't charge anybody. The choice of means to accomplish this is just as varied as the reason for the act. Some choose the quick, such as a firearm. Others the desperate and sick choose a painless way to reach their final decision like hanging or carbon monoxide poisoning. Some people find power tools an easily obtainable way to go because of their accessibility.

In this first case study is a young man in his early twenties. He has had problems at home with his parents. He wasn't doing well in school, lost his job and recently has broken up with his girlfriend. Most of us don't understand how the act of suicide is going to solve all this. Granted you no longer have to deal with your everyday problems but you can't start over and change yourself for the better either. We have our young man contemplating his life and his problems. He decides that his only recourse is to end his life, but how? After much thought he goes out to the garage and finds an electric hand drill. He looks around a little and finds a one inch wood boring bit. He puts it in the drill and tests it on a piece of wood. It works ok. He then takes a pencil and paper and starts writing done his reasons for committing this act, asks everyone for his forgiveness and tells them he loves them. At this point he places the left side of his head against the wall, places the drill bit against his right temple, pulls the power trigger and presses the dill into his head. He did manage to kill himself unfortunately not instantly. He passed out before he completed his task, fell to floor and slowly bleed to death which took several hours. What a desperate act from a desperate young man.

In our next case we have a similar but different scenario. Again we have a young man in his twenties. This young man is an Orthodox Hebrew. For those of you who don't know much about their religion I can tell you that it is very strict. It seems that our young man has strayed away from the religious rules. Instead of going to the synagogue as he said he was doing he was going to the local beach area and going to night clubs. He had started smoking and consuming alcohol. He even did these things on the Sabbath. Everything was going well until one evening when he got intoxicated, stole a car, drove intoxicated and crashed the vehicle into a tree in front of his house. Not knowing who was in the car, his parents called the local police. They responded to the scene and found our young man in the vehicle behind the wheel. He was uninjured but passed out. The police charged him with driving while intoxicated and car theft. He was released to his parents and a court date was scheduled. Needless to say he was quite embarrassed and his parents were shamed. The religious community attempted to help him and steer him back to the road of reprieve. It was much too much for him to bear. On the day of his court appearance he went across the street to a construction site where a new house was under constructed. The construction crew was on lunch break. He picked up a 7 ½" power circular saw, pulled back the blade guard and ran the spinning saw blade across his neck. He only lived a few moments after the act. He left behind a devastated family and community. Here again another desperate act from yet another desperate young man. In both of these cases our two victims thought they faced insurmountable circumstances and thought the only way to solve their problems was to take their own life. I've tried to find reasons to justify what they did but I don't know of any situation where death is the answer. If ever there was a reason it might involve sufferance from great pain or facing terminal illness. In the cases to follow this may be the case.

In our next case study we enter the area what can I do to help you? In this case we have an elderly women and her husband. The women had been suffering from a severe case of terminal cancer. She suffers daily. She has been taking medications for the pain but her cancer is so far advanced that the medications aren't really working. She sits daily and is lovingly taken care of by her husband to whom she has been married to 45 years. She begs him to help her die. She can't take the pain any longer. As much as he sees her pain he can't bring himself to honor her request. After a visit to her doctor her husband is told there is nothing else that can be done. Just try to make her as comfortable as possible. Her passing will be just a matter of time. He takes her home and she begs to die. Not being able to see her suffer any longer he goes out back to his work shed and picks up an electric nail gun. He goes back into the house and prepares lunch for his wife. She is in too much pain to eat. She is in tears an again asks him to relieve her of the pain. He looks at her and realizes that he can't bear to see her suffer any longer. He reluctantly picks up the nail gun, kisses her and tells her he loves her and fires six 4" nails into her head killing her instantly. He is devastated by his act. Not only has he killed his soul mate, he realizes that he can't live without her. He sits down and writes a note to his children telling them what he did and asks for their and God's forgiveness. He then sits in a chair next to his wife, grabs her hand and turns the nail gun on himself. He then fired five 4" nails into his heart. When they are found him he was still alive but in critical condition and unconscious. He was rushed to the hospital where he lives for four more days before he dies, a sad story. You start to ask yourself in cases like this about what would you do if you were faced with this situation. The case is considered a homicide / suicide. Some might call it a mercy killing. What about the remaining family? They lost both parents. Where were they when he needed help with her?

They may have been there; he may have refused their help. Elderly and illness and suicide, is it the only way?

The next case in this section is again another case of the elderly and illness. I realize this is sad, but it happens more than you think. We have a couple in their eighties living in a local retirement village. They have been residence in the community for about 15 years. They were well known and respected by their neighbors and friends. They were very active in community activities until one of them became ill. After what was thought to be a minor illness Mr. Ills found out that he had a terminal illness and that he had about a year to live. Mrs. Ills took care of him. They were no longer attending activities of the village and after a while their friends and neighbors learned of his illness. They would stop by now and then to visit. About a year after Mr. Ills was diagnosed with his illness Mrs. Ills went for her annual checkup and found that she had also contacted a terminal illness and she was given several months to live. Not wanting to burden their children with both of their illnesses they decided to commit suicide. They went into the garage, sat in the car and started it up. When they were found they were in the car with a bottle of wine and two glasses. They died in each other's arms. There was a note left behind to the children telling them not to grieve as they were both together and would be that way for eternity. Would this be enough to commit the ultimate act? I don't know. I guess it's something that you have to deal with when the time comes.

In our next case it's simply a case of fear. Our victim in this case is suffering with a severe tooth ache. According to his wife he has had a very bad tooth ache for over a month.

It had become so bad that at one time in the past month his cheek had swollen up. He even experiences a discharge from around his aching tooth. His wife begged for him to go to the dentist but he refused. He did however go to the hospital emergency room on a Saturday night complaining of facial pain. As you might expect the emergency room doctor told the man it was his tooth and he should go to the dentist. The victim stated that it was Saturday evening and he couldn't see the dentist until Monday. The emergency room doctor gave the man a prescription for an antibiotic and one for pain killers to hold him over until Monday. He filled the prescriptions, took them and by Monday was feeling better. The swelling was going down and the pain was gone. All is well right? Wrong five days later the pain was back and he was starting to swell again. His wife pled with him to call the dentist but he refused. Seeing that this was going nowhere fast his wife called the dentist, explained what happened and made an appointment for that late afternoon. Our victim was furious and said he wouldn't go but his wife insisted and he finally said ok. His wife said that she had to run out and do an errand and when she returned they would go to the dentist. He agreed. She left and he started thinking. He was afraid of the dentist and would rather have the pain then go. Then there was his wife. He thought for a while and decided to remove the tooth himself. How hard could it be? It was the answer he needed. He went to the garage and took out a pair of locking pliers. He took the pliers and tied them to the electric garage door opener. He needed help pulling out the tooth. He then clamped the pliers down on the tooth and pushed the open button on the door opening panel. The garage door opened and pulled the tooth from his jaw. His infection was so severe that when the tooth came out the tooth socket hemorrhaged. He tried to stop the bleeding but was unable too. He finally collapsed to the floor from the loss of blood. When his wife arrived back home from her errand she found the victim on the garage floor in a pool of blood. She called 911 but to no avail he bled to death before anyone could help him. I think my fear of death is worse than my fear of the dentist.

I really don't know how to classify this case. I mean it is homicide because she was trying to help. This case is one of the strangest I ever had to investigate. We have an elderly widowed woman in her eighties who lives in a retirement community with a live in health care worker. The health care worker has been with her since the death of the woman's husband. The health care worker was from Jamaica. She took care of all the woman's needs from cooking and cleaning to all her health care needs. There was a problem though the health care work practiced the occult. It seemed that the health care worker feared the spirit of the women's dead husband. She said the winds of his spirit were heavy around her legs. To compensate for this the health care worker made the sign of the cross on all the pictures of the deceased husband in the house in olive oil. She also spread salt around the entire interior perimeter of the residence to try to keep the spirit winds out. She feared that the spirit would inhibit the wife and drag her to the dark side of the spirit world. She was determined to save her. She turned to her bible and to her religion. She said her religion was Santeria. In a last ditch effort to save the woman the health care worker removed the woman's eyes with the aid of poultry shears while the woman was still alive. This saved here soul from the dark side spirits. As a result of this action the elderly woman bled to death. The health care worker called the family and told them that the woman passed away. Family members came to house to find the woman neatly dressed and lying on the bedroom floor next to the bed. Nothing seemed out of place and everything was neat and clean. The only thing that stuck out as strange was a sizable blood stain in the carpet near the woman's feet. They called police. Responding officers didn't think at first that fowl play may have been at work but just to be safe called for the crime scene unit. Upon our arrival we examined the scene and the victim and determined this to be a homicide because of the lack evidence. In addition when the health care worker was being questioned she rolled her eyes and collapsed. She was taken to the hospital where she was placed under observation. Several attempts to question her always ended up the same way with her passing out. We weren't aware that the women's eyes were missing until we received a call from the autopsy detectives who told us her eyes were removed. We search the entire house for the women's eyes. Due to the absence of blood we chose to examine the residence with a chemical called Luminol. Luminol is a chemical solution that reacts with hemoglobin's. Hemoglobin's are oxygen carrying proteins in the blood. When the Luminol is contacted with the hemoglobin's a light producing chemical reaction occurs called chemilumiesence. This is the same thing that happens to fire flies and light sticks when they glow. Luminol must be used in the dark in order to see the reaction. After we darkened the room we sprayed the Luminol solution to the interior of the residence room by room starting where the victim was located. As the Luminol was applied we saw a glowing reaction from the victim's body location to the bathroom door that led to the bedroom. I have to add at this time that with the lights on the bathroom and the rest of the residence appeared clean and neat with no visible signs of blood anywhere except the one blood stain next to the body. As we entered the bathroom with the Luminol the fluorescent reaction was overwhelming. The bathroom lit up like there were lights turned on. Apparently the health care worker cleaned up the bathroom but invisible residues remained. One downside of Luminol is that it also reacts with fats. Most cleaning detergents are made from animal fats. We went from the bathroom out into the hall. In the hall, into the living room, across the dining room, into the kitchen and laundry room where we observed a trail of right foot marks leading from the bathroom to the laundry room. A search was undertaken throughout the residence and one of the victim's eyes was recovered inside the washing machine. We also found some washed wet clothing in the washing machine.

An investigation of the healthcare workers room turned up several items of the occult that we weren't familiar with. One of the local officer said he knew of a so called priestess in town. We sent two detectives with the officer to speak to her about our findings. They returned a short time later with information that was startling. The things that we found in the health care workers room were used in the practice of Voodoo. The priestess also said that if the woman was sacrificed to save her soul that in addition to her eyes being removed we would find three coins lying close to the woman's body face up. The coins were found along with salt and olive oil. After a psychiatric evaluation the health care worker was cleared for trial. She eventually confessed to killing the women however still stuck to her story of that she was saving the women's soul from the spirit dark side. She was sentenced to 30 years to life in prison without being eligible for parole for a minimum of 30 years.

In this next case we have an elderly woman living by herself in a retirement community. Her daughter stops over daily to take care of her and her needs. The woman is in her 80's and very frail. On this day in particular the daughter took her mother to the doctor for a checkup. On the way home they stopped at the market to get a few items and then went home. When they reached the house the woman went inside while her daughter emptied the car and brought in the items they bought. She placed them on the floor and went to close the car door.

When she returned her mother was lying on the floor. She had attempted to pick up a bag from the floor and fell to the floor. The daughter immediately leaned over and picked her up. She sat her in a chair. The elderly woman said that she had chest pain and was having a difficult time breathing. Her daughter immediately called 911. Police and paramedics arrived and took the woman to the hospital but the woman died at the hospital upon arrival. An autopsy was performed the next day and the medical examiner determined the cause of death to be a laceration to the left lung by a broken rib and listed the manner of death as suspicious. He remarked that there was no sign of trauma to the injured area. Further investigation showed that the woman's rib was broken by the daughter when she picked her up from the floor. They originally charged the daughter with manslaughter but the charge was dropped due to the extreme brittle bone condition of the woman.

CHAPTER FOUR

All In The Name Of Love

In this chapter we will explore the concept of I love him or her so much that I will kill them to keep them from not loving me and other acts in the name of love. This is what some people really think. It sounds bazaar and weird but it happens more often than you think and their reason for doing this are just as weird.

In this first case we have a married couple living in an upper middle class section of town. They have a nice home in a very nice neighborhood. They have two children in their middle teens. Our story starts out as your normal couple. I won't go as far as to say everything was perfect as it was not. No relationship is perfect. We all have some problems at one time or another. Our couple's problems stem mostly from alcohol. They both enjoy a drink and enjoy it frequently. The problem is that when they consume alcohol they change. This happens to many people. Our couple has experienced some problems in the past because of their drinking. It has gotten to a point where their drinking has at times upgraded to domestic violence. The police had been called to settle a dispute in the past. In our most recent incident our husband comes home from work after stopping off with the guys for a couple of beers. Of course he didn't call or expect to stay as long as he did. Upon arriving home his wife is upset because dinner was ready an hour ago. She voices her feelings about him not being on time. She says that the children have already eaten and went out with their friends. He immediately gets on the defensive and there you have it an argument. As the argument goes on it gets louder and louder. The words get meaner and meaner. Both of them lose their tempers. She throws the dinner at him. He gets even more upset and smashes the glass doors to the patio. In doing so he causes a piece of glass to strike her on arm. She has a minor cut that starts to bleed. While all this was going on a neighbor hears the noise and calls the police. The police arrive and hear the yelling coming from inside the house. They enter the house, separate the husband and wife and start asking each of them what caused the argument. They both explain their side of the story. In the process of questioning the two people one of the officer's notices that the wife is cut and bleeding. The cut is minor and doesn't require any major first aid but she is bleeding. The officers are now required by law to place the husband under arrest even though he didn't intentionally cut her. She is cut however through an act which he instituted so he must be taken into custody. He is taken to police headquarters where he is charged with domestic violence. Police fill out their report and take the husband to the county jail where he is placed into lockup awaiting appearance before the judge in the morning. His bail is set at $5000.00 with a 10% option. That means his bail is $5000.00 but the court will accept $500.00 in good faith and release him as he doesn't have a prior record. He is allowed to make phone calls to try to raise the bail. Who do you think he calls? You guessed it, his wife. Feeling bad about what happened she agrees to bail him out. She calls her neighbor and asks him to take her to the court house to bail out her husband because she is too upset to drive. He says ok and off they go. Once released from jail they go home with the neighbor driving.

When they get home it's pretty late. They go upstairs, take a shower and go to bed. Both of them say they are sorry, kiss and make up by having sex. Afterwards she goes downstairs to get a glass of juice. He follows her down and opens a beer. They sit and talk for a while. He has another beer and she joins him. One beer leads to another and after a while it starts all over again. This time however the argument is over why she had the neighbor's husband drive her to the court house and not his wife. She says that she called the neighbor and asked for a ride because she was upset. The neighbor said she was helping her children with their homework but she would have her husband take her. He doesn't believe her. He said that she invited him over as soon as he was taken to jail. He asks her just what she was doing. She says that she wasn't doing anything. He calls her a liar, reaches across the table, slaps her and calls her a slut. She stands up and hits him with a beer bottle. They begin to physically fight each other. She still has the bottle and hits him two more times. In his rage he picks up a steak knife off the kitchen counter and stabs her in the chest several times. She falls to the floor crying and bleeding very badly and dies. He falls to the floor after realizing what he has done and tries to save her but he cannot. He is scared and intoxicated. He thinks about his situation and comes to the conclusion that he will go to jail for the rest of his life. Not wanting to go to jail he takes the steak knife and plunges it into the side of his neck. He then lies down on the floor next to his wife and dies alongside the woman he loves.

Just as it happened before a neighbor calls the police after hearing the yelling and screaming. The arriving officers enter the home only to find the two of them dead on the kitchen floor in their underwear in a large pool of blood. While the police were there the children arrived home but the police didn't allow them to enter the home and called for relatives to come and take the children. This is something that happens all too often. Domestic violence is a crime that occurs often and it often causes other crimes to occur.

This crime scene is a forensic nightmare. I told you the story of how this crime occurred but we didn't know what happened until after we processed the scene. It sounds pretty cut and dry at first sight but what if he didn't stab her or himself. Could it be possible that someone else stabbed her when she came down stairs? He hears the noise and goes down to investigate, sees the actor, confronts him and ends up getting stabbed in the neck in the process. These questions can't be answered until the scene is processed. Blood samples must be taken from all over the scene. Fingerprint processing must be done to see if any prints not belonging to the persons occupying the home are found. Evidence must be collected and tested.

The things we found were only the victim's blood. The wives fingerprints were on the beer bottle. The husband's fingerprints were on the knife. The doors were locked when the police arrived. No signs of forced entry. Nothing was missing or stolen. By a systematic examination we eliminated all possible scenarios until we were left with the one of homicide / suicide which was a result of a domestic violence.

In this next case we have another case of domestic violence. It was a Sunday morning when our father went to the home of his ex-wife to take his 8 year old son out for the day. It was his day for visitation. They also have a 2 year but she is too small to be taken out all day. Just like every other Sunday he would take his son to the park or to the movies. On this day in particular while they were at the park his son said to his father that mommy has a new boyfriend. He also told his father that his mother's new boyfriend kissed her on the lips. At the end of his visitation he returned the child to his ex-wife and left without incident. While home he began thinking about what his son had told him. His head was spinning. He was mad. He was sad. He was confused. When it reached a point where he couldn't take it anymore he went into his kitchen and picked up a 14" knife. He took the knife, got into his car and drove to the home of his ex-wife. When he arrived at his ex-wife's home he knocked on the door. She opened the door to see what he wanted. At that point he drew the knife. She immediately ran upstairs where the children were. He chased her up the stairs and into the bedroom. The 2 year old was in her playpen at the top of the stairs and his son was in his room. When she got to her room she picked up the telephone and dialed the police. The emergency operator tried to get information from the woman but only could hear her screaming and begging for her life. He entered the room behind her and began stabbing her as she was calling the police. He stabbed her numerous times during an altercation that caused all the bedroom furniture to be moved. Finally she lay lifeless on the floor. As he turned to leave the room he noticed that his 8 year old son watching what happened from the bathroom door which accessed the bedroom. He turned toward his son, knife in hand, and approached the bathroom. The young boy slammed the door shut and locked it. His father tried to push the door open and yelled to the boy to unlock the door. He didn't. Our actor then realized that there was also access to the bathroom from the hallway outside the bedroom. He turned toward the hallway and left the room. The young boy also realized that there was a door to the bathroom in the hallway. He rushed to the door to lock it but his father got there at the same time. The boy pushed the door in an effort to close it while his father pushed from the other side to open it to get to the boy. The boy fell to the floor and pushed his feet against the bottom of the door holding it and keeping his father out. After a short time our actor left the house. The eight year old boy waited until he was sure his father had left and then went into the bedroom to help his mother but it was too late. He then took his 2 year old sister out of the playpen and took her across the street to the home of his uncle his mother's bother. It was starting to snow. The young boy and his sister got to their uncle's home and the boy told his uncle that his father had stabbed his mother real bad and she was on the bedroom floor. The uncle rushed across the street to the home. He went upstairs and found his dead sister lying on the bloody floor half naked and stabbed severely to the chest, neck, abdomen and legs. He looked for the telephone but it was ripped from the wall and covered in blood. He went downstairs and telephoned the police from down there. At about the same time this was happening our actor was entering the police department. He walked up to the window and told the desk sergeant that he had just killed his ex-wife. He was holding the bloody 14" knife and he was covered in blood. Sounds like a fairly easy case to close but determinations had to be made as to whether it was a crime of passion or a premeditated homicide. You ask what difference does it make homicide is homicide. Well when it comes to sentencing there is a big difference. In a crime of passion you can be sentenced to a prison term of 5 years. If it is a premeditated homicide you can be sentenced for 30 years to life or even receive a death penalty. It was necessary for the crime scene investigators to determine the difference with evidence. I will explain what I mean. I described the circumstances of the crime in the beginning of this case. At the time of the investigation we didn't know where the knife came from. If our actor went to the house to confront her about the new boyfriend and during the course of the discussion became upset and in a rage of passion picked up the knife that was closely at hand and stabbed his ex-wife it could be reviewed as a crime of passion. Remember our actor went to the police with the knife, confessed and turned himself in. This all adds to his being sorry and showing remorse. However, during the investigation we didn't find any knives in the residence that matched the knife he used. We did find a matching set of knives at his home. In addition forensically we showed that he brought the knife to the victim's home by carrying it in his back pants pocket. The pocket was cut where the knife had been. It was also the same pocket he put the knife in to take it to the police department. We made that determination by the blood stain inside the pocket. This was proof enough to show that he brought the knife from home to the crime scene with the intent of using it on his ex-wife. Just a quick note here, if you remember in the beginning I mentioned that the size of the crime scene could be large or small. In this case we had the scene of the crime in addition to the actor's home which was six miles away. His home also became part of the crime scene. In this case the actor pled out to homicide in return for a 30 year to life sentence with no eligibility of parole for 30 years to avoid a trial with the prosecution seeking the death penalty. Life always seems to be the better choice.

In the next case we examine the love between two sisters. Let me set the scene. Two elderly sisters live together in a retirement community. They have lived together for over 20 years. Both are widows and took up residence together so as not to have to live their lives out alone in an empty house. They were very close and were always together. They went to club meetings together. They involved themselves together in everything they did from grocery shopping to Bingo. As things happen in life one of the sister developed terminal cancer. For the last three years of their existence together the sister who was well took care of her sick sister. She fed her, bathe her, took her to the doctors. Whatever was needed she did for her stricken sister. Sadly one day the cancer stricken sister had a stroke and was given weeks to a month to live. She begged for her sister to save her from the pain she was suffering from the cancer. She would plead with her to take her life. As the days went by the pain became worse and worse to a point where one day she could no longer watch her sister suffer and agreed to help her end her life. She gave her a kiss good bye, placed a pillow over her face and held it there until she stopped breathing. She was devastated by the event and relieved that her sister would suffer no more. Now she was faced with a new problem. How could she explain her sister's death? To make matters worse a home health care nurse would be there in the morning 12 hours away. Then she thought I'll call the police in the morning and tell them that she died in her sleep.

When morning came she got up, called police and told them that she thought her sister had died during the night. They said that they would send an officer right over. Just as she hung up the phone the home health care worker arrived. She examined the sister and confirmed that she in fact had died. The police arrived and spoke to the sister and health care worker. The health care worker told the officer that something didn't seem right. When asked what she meant she remarked that the dead woman wasn't lying on a pillow. The pillow was alongside her. The officer asked the sister if this was normal and she said yes she always slept that way. The officer thought that the sister responded strangely and requested that crime scene and the medical examiner be notified. Crime scene arrived first and took an over view of the scene. They noticed a brownish stain on the underside of the pillow lying alongside the dead sister. They also noticed that only one dinner plate was in the sink from the evening before but that there were two lunch plates from that day in the sink. Further examination of the body showed petechial hemorrhaging. Petechial hemorrhaging is a condition when blood escapes from the blood vessel and forms on the surface of the tissue, in this case the whites of the eyes. This condition is very common in strangulation and suffocation. The medical examiner arrived and confirmed the suspicions of the crime scene investigator. The woman was found in the face up position. Photographs and video were taken. The pillow was taken into evidence and the victim's body was bagged and sealed and taken to the morgue for an autopsy. At the autopsy the pathologist confirmed that the 89 year old victim was suffocated. Her 86 year old sister was taken into custody and charged with homicide. The stain on the pillowcase was saliva and further DNA testing confirmed it was the victim's. This is a very sad case and unfortunately doesn't end here. The sister of the victim was charged with homicide and confessed. Due to her age the court chose not to send her to prison but placed her under house arrest for 5 years. During this time she attempted suicide twice and succeeded on her second attempt. She left a note to relatives saying that she was sorry for what she had done but did not regret it. She also said now she and her sister would be together again.

This next case takes doing it yourself to a whole new level. Our victim in this case is a well-respected business man. He has a very profitable electrical construction business. Along with this he is a gun enthusiast and collector. On this particular day he is in his garage with his latest addition to his firearms collection, a practice hand grenade. It's a real hand grenade that doesn't have any gun powder in it. Of course he wasn't happy with this. He wanted to make it active and take it to a range to explode it. He figured out that it couldn't be that difficult. Hand grenades are basically a hollowed out piece of metal. The metal is scored and grooved in such a way that upon exploding the metal comes apart into many small fragments called shrapnel. These fragments travel at high velocity in all directions. This is what causes the damage. Our victim figured out that all he had to do to make the grenade work was to fill it with gun powder. This task was made easy by simply by unscrewing the top portion of the grenade. Then fill it with gun powder. The top portion of a hand grenade contains the fuse that ignites the gun powder when the pin is pulled out of the handle. The handle ejects and strikes the fuse causing a spark. This spark is what sets off the powder. Our victim had a can of gun powder in the garage which he used in the past to reload his own ammunition. He unscrewed the fuse portion of the hand grenade removed it and filled the hand grenade with the gun powder. He did some research into how much powder to put into the hand grenade. He measured it out and put it into the empty metal grenade. He then screwed the fuse section back into the top of the grenade. This however was the part where he should have done a little more research. Gun powder is very unstable and must be handled with extreme care. As our victim was screwing the fuse section back into the hand grenade he neglected to wipe the excess gun powder from the threads of the hand grenade. As he twisted the fuse section into the metal hand grenade the two metal parts rubbed against each other. The gun powder residue in the threads was ignited by the friction caused by the two metal parts grinding together. He was holding the hand grenade in his left hand and against this body. While holding the grenade in his left hand he screwed the fuse section on with his right hand pressing the sections together. As a result of the explosion he was blown into numerous pieces which went in all directions and decorated the garage from floor to ceiling. On the wall was a very large patriotic sign that read

"God, Guns and Guts Built America". His guts became part of that sign. This wasn't a crime scene in the full sense of the word. Actually it was an accidental death. The problem was where did the hand grenade come from? We started an investigation to determine the legality of the firearms, gun powder and hand grenade.

CHAPTER FIVE

I'll Show Her

In almost 22 years of investigating crime and death scenes I've learned some very interesting things. One of these interesting things is why most men commit the act of suicide. Usually it's what I call the "I'll Show Her" reason. In suicide writings left behind most actors describe the reasons for what they have done. The reasons vary as you might guess but more often than not it has something to do with a female. In his state of mind at the time he fails to look at one fact. By eliminating himself from the situation he isn't solving anything. Actually if it's a situation where they are splitting up instead of her getting half she now gets it all. How does he win?

In this first case we have an 18 year old young man. He thinks his whole life is a waste and his only solution is to take his own life. This will make everything better in his mind. On a late summer evening he decides it's time to fix everything. He takes a rope, gets on his bicycle and rides to a nearby bridge that crosses from the mainland to the beach community in which he resides. At the bridge he peddles about half way up the bridge. He leaves the bicycle and walks the remaining two hundred yards to the top of the bridge. He ties one end of the rope to the bridge and makes a noose on the other end.

He then places the noose around neck, climbs over the side of the bridge which is about 70 feet over the water and jumps. Sounds simple right? Well I guess when everything isn't going your way why should this? Because he made a noose in the end of the rope when he jumped the noose loosened and slid off his neck and went across his face. Because of the rope ending up where it did his face was crushed in and he suffered for hours before he died. If the rope had been placed around his neck his death would have been swift. However there is also the chance that he could have been decapitated if the rope was around his neck. In that case his body would have fallen into the water and not have been found for days and his head may never have been found. His body was discovered by a motorist driving across an adjacent bridge in the opposite direction that was only 10 feet from the water. As I approached the scene from the lower bridge I saw the victim hanging from the other bridge. I made a U-turn at the end of the bridge and drove up to the scene on the other bridge. I walked up to the rail and thought all this was a hoax. It didn't look real from the top of the bridge looking down. Below the victim there was a police boat and the boat officers said it was a body because it was bleeding. We pulled the rope up to retrieve the victim but were unable to. We decided to attach another rope to the victim's rope then cut his rope from the bridge and lower him to the boat below, which we did. The boat officers took the victim to the shore where he was examined by the medical examiner and pronounced dead. We checked the victim's pockets to see if we could identify him. Along with his wallet was a piece of paper that had a suicide note written to his girlfriend. The note to his girlfriend read "It's not my fault. I lost my job. My mom threw me out and you don't love me anymore. Now you can be happy." He showed her!

This next case took time and planning right down to the selection of music used. Here we are again with another young man. This actor is 19 years old. He has been out on his own for about a year after he decided that he just couldn't conform to the rules at home set by his parents. After all he was 19 and a grown man. He would make his own rules. Well things didn't go exactly as planned. He had a job but lost it because he was unable to get to work on time. He actually had a couple of jobs that he lost for one reason or another. He had an apartment but because of losing his job he lost his apartment. He was living with his girlfriend at the apartment but when they could no longer pay the rent she decided to move back home. This presented other problems for him because her parents didn't like him so seeing her was difficult. She would make excuses to get to go see him. To make matters worse she had met someone new. He was 2 years older, had a great job and was well liked by her parents. She liked him too. The thing that brought everything to this point in his life was when she said that she couldn't see our victim anymore because she was pregnant and the baby wasn't his. Feeling the pressure he comes to the conclusion that suicide was his only way out.

Being an inventive young man and not being able to express in words how he is feeling he decides to make a sound recording of his feelings. He gets two cassette tape players. On one tape player he plays a song called "Suicide Relief" which plays over and over. On the other cassette player he records his feelings and his reasons for this tragic act. He blames his now ex-girlfriend and says he knows that the baby is his but she won't admit it because of her parents. After recording his reasons and feelings he proceeds to do the deed. He goes as far as to explain step by step what he is doing. It goes something like this. I'm moving the chair under the hanging lamp. I'm now tying the rope to the lamp. I'm standing on the chair with the rope around my neck. I guess this is it. I hope you'll remember me and tell my baby about its father. Ok this it! (Keep in mind that the music is still playing) He says "goodbye" and kicks out the chair. Just then there is a tremendous crash. He says "damn the rope broke". After much shuffling he reconstructs the scene and tries again. This time he succeeds.

Let's change gears here. This next case is quite different. We have a married couple who have been on the road to divorce for a long time. The only problem is that neither one of them wants to leave the house. Their situation is unique. They both sleep in separate rooms. They cook their own meals and pay their own personal bills. They do jointly pay bills pertaining to the home. The usual things mortgage, electric, water, taxes and telephone. One of these items will be what brings this separate living paradise to its conclusion. One evening while watching television together, the wife of this relationship is in the process of paying the household bills. She methodically goes through them one by one. From time to time she converses with her husband on certain items. When she gets to the telephone bill he asks how much the bill was. She tells him the amount and he says isn't that a little high. She says if it is, it's because of all the calls your making. He immediately takes the offensive and says he doesn't make any calls. She makes them all. She denies his accusations and says that he is always on the phone. He says only because everyone calls him he doesn't call anybody. He goes on to say it's because she is always calling her mother. The words get stronger and stronger and meaner and meaner. Finally he says that's enough just pay the bill and gets up from his chair and goes to his room. She is sitting there reading the telephone bill when he returns from his room. She says look right here all of these calls are yours. He glares at her and takes a .357 mag pistol out from under his shirt and shoots here six times point blank range in the chest. The bullets actually go right through the telephone bill. He takes the gun into the kitchen and empties the spent casings into the trash. He then reloads the gun goes into the living room, lies down on the couch and puts the pistol in his mouth and pulls the trigger.

The police are called to the house because family members have been unable to contact the couple. They didn't answer the telephone or the door. They force open the door and find the wife sitting up in the chair with her head down as if she nodded off. She had six gunshot wounds in the center of her chest. The telephone bill was still in her hand. The husband was lying on the couch across from his wife with the back of his head blown out. The pistol was still in his hand.

During the crime scene investigation we found quite a few guns hidden in various places throughout the house. She had as many hidden guns as he did. At least the bills were paid.

I know that the name of this chapter is "I'll Show Her" but fair is fair. Here's an "I'll Show Him" case. This is one of things that you just can't figure out why they happen. Our couple is your upper middle class couple. Everything is great. Good family, plenty of money, beautiful home and all the extras we all would like to have. Our husband had a great business and worked hard. He finally decided that he had enough money and sold his business and retired. He went out and bought a large 48' fishing boat and ran fishing charters as a small business. Our wife was a business woman who retired about the same time as her husband. She kept busy with the children and friends and running a small business on the computer.

On the day in question our husband had a fishing charter and left the house around 5:00 am. Before leaving he said goodbye to his wife. She asked him if on the way home to stop and pick up some bags for the vacuum cleaner. He said ok and left. When she got up she had coffee and then left to have breakfast with her daughter. She returned late morning, did a little computer work and then decided to go do some shopping. She got into her Mercedes S-Class and drove off.

It was late afternoon when her husband comes back in from his fishing charter. He cleaned up the boat and put all the gear away. He left the dock and headed home. On his way home he stopped off at the local store and bought vacuum cleaner bags. When he returned to the house his wife hadn't returned yet. He went into the computer room to check the answering machine and computer to see if he had any new charters. He was there for about an hour when his wife arrived home. She seemed to be upset about something. She walked into the computer room and asked what he thought he was doing. He said he was checking to see if there were any new charters. She started yelling that all he ever thought about was his boat. She told him to get off the computer that it was for her business and for him to go get his own.

He said I bought the computer and I'll use it anytime I want. The argument continued. They weren't yelling but they were arguing. He finally told her he would get off the computer when he was done. She stormed out of the room talking to herself loudly as she went. He was still on the computer when she came back into the room. She told him to get up and when he didn't she told him that he bought the wrong vacuum bags and shot him six times and killed him. She then went into the kitchen to make something to eat and left the house. Their daughter arrived a short time later and found her father dead on the computer room floor and called police. When the police arrived they found the scene as the daughter had. One other thing they found was a note taped to the vacuum cleaner that said wrong bags. The wife was found returning home from the store. She went out to get vacuum cleaner bags.

This case will really get into things in depth, literally. Here we are with a couple who have lived together for several years. He was a painter and she was a homemaker. She had a son and daughter from a previous marriage. Her son was mentally challenged and at times got violent. Our happy couple had just returned from vacation on which they took a cruise to the Caribbean. About a week after the vacation she decides that their relationship really wasn't going anywhere so when he came home from work she told him that it was over and that she wanted him to move out. This was a shock to him. He tried to ask why and what bought this on but she kept saying you have to leave. He already had stress problems and this wasn't helping him any. He was under a doctor's care and was on Prozac for depression. She insisted that he sleep on the couch until he was able to find another place to live.

Another week goes by and she is still telling him to leave. On that evening he goes to sleep on the couch but can't sleep. He finally decides that if he can't have her nobody can. He goes into the kitchen and takes a large kitchen knife from the wood knife block on the counter. He goes down the hall and enters her bedroom. Without hesitation he leans over her as she slept. She was sleeping on her back in the center of her king sized water bed. He takes one last look at her and plunges the knife into her chest. She is startled and wakes. He continues to stab her over and over again. She tries to fight him off but he is much stronger the she is. He keeps stabbing her until she lay lifeless on the bed. He then leaves the room and is met in the hallway by her son. He asked him where he is going and where is his mother? He tells the boy that she is tired and sleeping late and that he was going to go to the bakery to get some donuts for breakfast. He gets in his truck and drives off. Remember this spot in the story.

Now that he has killed his girlfriend and left the residence he's confused as what to do next. His guilt gets to him so he drives to police headquarters. He walks in and tells in detail what he has done. The police respond and find everything as it was left except that the victim's son is now standing in the hallway covered with blood and is noticeable upsct and yelling obscenities at the officers. They have to physically subdue him and remove him from the home. He is taken to a local hospital where he can be treated. They examine the house for any other persons and call the crime scene unit. Upon our arrival at the scene we found the victim in the middle of the bed on her back. She was stabbed numerous times. The autopsy would tell us that she was actually stabbed 96 times. On the bed next to the victim was the murder weapon, the large knife from the kitchen. The tip of the knife was bent probably from striking a bone during the attack. The amazing thing about this homicide was that he stabbed the victim 96 times with enough force to actually bend the tip of the knife. Of the 96 stab wounds at least 70 of the wounds completely penetrated her body from front to back. Here's the amazing part, the water bed wasn't punctured, not even once. Our killer had excellent depth control. The actor pled guilty and received a 30 year to life sentence with no chance of parole for 30 years. I go back to the victim's son. If the actor hadn't walked into police headquarters and said he killed his girlfriend it's very possible that the son could have been a suspect in the homicide. He had a history of mental illness, assault and, violence. When we looked into his room we saw that he had kicked and punched holes in all the sheetrock in the room. Also remember that when the police arrived he was in the hallway covered in blood. As it turned out we got the right man. He showed her.

This next case was in the national spotlight. It's really not your usual "I'll show her" it's more of a "We'll show him" case. The notoriety of this case even prompted the writing of a book and the making of a movie as well. You may or may not recall it. Our actor is a very successful business man in town. He has all the things everyone else wants. He has a beautiful wife, three wonderful children, a nice home, cars etc. You get the picture so what makes him want to throw it all away? Only he can answer that question. He enjoyed going to Atlantic City, NJ with his wife for dinner and would do so often. He was on an ego trip however. Basically he was a showoff. He was the type of person who would ask for a telephone to be brought to the table in a restaurant just to be noticed. It was that way with everything he did.

I said that he had everything going for him and blew it. He found himself a girlfriend on the side and took up with her quite often. He said that he fell in love with her and was willing to give up everything else to have her but before he did this he took out a million dollar insurance policy on his wife. One evening he met this man from Louisiana at a party. He was talking to him and told him about the situation he was in and mentioned that if his wife was dead everything would be perfect. He could keep everything he already has, keep the new girlfriend and have a million dollars from his wife's insurance policy too. As the conversation went on he asked the man from Louisiana if he knew of anybody in Louisiana who would do something like this for some quick cash. Then they joked about it and the Louisiana man said I'll ask around and call you. They exchanged telephone numbers and ended their conversation.

A couple of weeks later our devoted husband received a call from the man in Louisiana who told him he had a couple of guys who were interested in helping him with his situation. He said that he would have them contact him and our husband said ok. It didn't take long when our husband gets a telephone call from the Louisiana man's friend. They discussed money and possible scenarios for taking care of the business at hand. The new Louisiana contact said that he would like to come to New Jersey and take a look at the things they discussed and see different areas where the task could be accomplished. He also said he had a partner who would help him. The husband agreed and a date was set for the man to come to New Jersey. A week or so later they met as agreed and formulated a plan. It was set, the date was picked. Our husband was elated everything would soon be fine.

On the date selected our husband has a reservation to have dinner with his wife in Atlantic City. They go to dinner as they have on many occasions. They depart Atlantic City and as they are driving home he says to his wife I have to pull over I think there is something wrong with the tire. There is a rest stop up ahead and he pulls in. The rest stop is dimly lit. He pulls around to the side of the rest area and gets out. He walks over to the tire to see what is wrong. At that point a man approaches the passenger side of the car and shoots the women twice. Just then the husband is struck on the head and is knocked out. He awakes, sees his wife shot and runs out to the roadway for help and to get the police. When the police arrive he relates that same story to them and an investigation is started. The crime scene unit processes the scene and the car. An autopsy is performed and two bullets are recovered. Everything seems ok as far as homicides go except one thing a million dollar insurance policy that was taken out a week before the incident. The other factor is our grieving husband is not so grieving. He goes to his office, stops off with business associates and sees his girlfriend almost every day. The investigation continues for weeks. During this time he brings his girlfriend to the house and introduces her to his sons. During the investigation it's discovered that our husband has made several telephone calls to Louisiana and has received just as many from there. They investigated the calls and saw that one was to a man under investigation by the FBI. They talk to the husband's first Louisiana contact and manage to get a name from him of the other Louisiana contact. When they talk to this man they see something is wrong and pursue the interrogation and finally the man confesses but not to killing the woman only setting up the killing with the husband. He also gives up the name of a man that he says is the shooter. All four men are arrested for conspiracy to commit homicide and homicide and are all jailed. The Louisiana man who confessed to the detectives agreed to testify for the state and receive a lesser sentence. The others will stand trial. All along the man accused of being the shooter claimed his innocence. He said I couldn't have been here and I never talked to anybody about any murder. It took about two years to go to trial and when it did the man who testified for the state told his story. The man accused of shooting the woman said that he was at the dentist office with his son and there wasn't any way possible he could have been here to shoot the women. The original Louisiana contact with the husband claimed his innocence stating all I did was set up a couple of telephone calls connecting two men. He had been offered a plea bargain to testify on behalf of the state against the husband and be credited with his time already served, about a year and released. He would have to plead guilty to conspiracy to commit homicide and hc would be released. He said I'm not guilty, I didn't do anything and I won't make plea that I did.

The court checked out the story the accused shooter told and found it to be exactly as he had said. He was released from custody and acquitted. The informer who testified for the state received a 5 year sentence and was released after serving 18 months in jail. The go between who claimed innocents was convicted of conspiracy to commit homicide and was sentenced to 30 years to life without parole eligibility for 30 years. Our husband who had it all figured out was sentence to the death penalty. His sentence was commuted to life without parole. I would say that could be called "We showed him".

CHAPTER SIX

You Can Run But You Can't Hide!

In this chapter there will be quite a mixture of cases where criminals initially get away with the crime but get caught in the end. One of the common crimes committed on a daily basis is burglary. Burglary, sometimes called breaking and entering or housebreaking is the illicit intrusion or entry into an area for the express purpose of theft. In this first case the actor approaches a residence where the occupants are not home. He goes around the rear of the house. He puts on gloves and cuts the screen open on the rear window leading into the kitchen. He then forces open the locked window with a pry bar. He climbs in the window and proceeds to look through the home for anything of value he can sell. He finds a jar with cash in it in the kitchen. He also finds several pieces of jewelry upstairs in the bedroom. He fills his pockets with his find and continues looking around the house. He opens drawers, cabinet and closets. Taking whatever he can and putting it in his pockets he goes back into the kitchen and climbs back out the window in the rear where he entered and leaves. Seems like everything went according to plan and he got away with the perfect crime.

Why the perfect crime, well nobody saw him, he wore gloves so we don't have fingerprints and he sells the proceeds to a fence (another criminal who disposes of the goods for him). The victim's arrive home to discover that they have been burglarized. They call the police who respond, take a report and call the crime scene unit. The crime scene unit processes the scene as we described earlier with photographing, fingerprinting etc. Our actor wore gloves so he doesn't get any prints. One thing was found however that will help the police. Our actor was so intent in stuffing his pockets with loot that in the process he dropped his wallet. That kind of makes it easy, wallet, name, address, everything. Gotcha!

In this next case we have an actor who lets his wife go to work while he sits home and watches television. It seems that there isn't anything good on television so in his boredom he decides to take a walk around the neighborhood. They live in a bungalow in a beach community. It's off season so there aren't a lot of people around especially during the day on a week day. He walks around until he finds another bungalow that seems inviting. He walks around it carefully checking all the doors and windows to see if any are open or unlocked. He is also checking to see if anyone else is around. Not seeing anybody he goes around to the back of the house and forces open the rear door with a screwdriver he just happen to bring with him. He enters the house and begins to search for anything worth stealing. The house is really pretty empty. The owners live in another part of the state and only come to the house in the summer months. He opens a closet and sees a large glass bowl filled with pennies. It's very heavy. He looks around and takes a pillow case from the linen closet and dumps the pennies from the bowl into the pillow case. He then takes the bag of pennies and throws it over his shoulder, leaves out the rear door and goes back home, about three blocks away.

During a routine patrol a police officer drives through the neighborhood as part of his normal duties and sees the rear door of the bungalow open. He gets out of the car to investigate and notices that there are pry marks on the door and door frame. He calls the crime scene unit to process the scene. They photograph the scene and while photographing the door and door frame the detective notices several pennies on the floor and on the door sill. He turns and looks behind him and sees that the trail of pennies leads off between the houses. He gets the officer who found the scene and the two of them head off following the penny trail. The trail leads them to the actor's bungalow. They knock on the door. He answers and asks them what they want. They ask to come in and he lets them in. Sitting in the corner on the floor is the pillow case full of pennies. Hansel and Gretel would be proud.

Not everyone has to be an adult to be a burglar. Next we have two juveniles. Two boys, one 11 years old and the other 12 years old. They live in a waterfront community. Some of the residents live in the area year round while others are only seasonal residence. The two boys are year round residents. Half of the houses on the street that boys live on are unoccupied during the winter months. I have to give you a little background before we can continue. These boys and the resident of the scene have had problems in the past. Our victim has chased the boys from in front of his house numerous times because they are too loud. The victim has even gone as far as to call the police on them on one occasion.

Our story starts on a Saturday in the winter. Its cold out and the boys are bored. They walk down the street to the victim's house and go around to the rear of the building. There aren't any occupied residences on this end of the street. When they reach the back of the house they kick open the screen door to the porch and then force open the rear door to the house and enter. The door leads them into the living room where they start kicking over tables and furniture. They find some Champaign, open it, take off their jackets and drink some. They then enter the dining room area and smash the china closet and china and glassware. They pour other bottles of liquor they found all around the dining room. Next stop is the kitchen where they empty cabinets all over the floor. Spice bottles are opened and dumped out. Bottles of liquids from the refrigerator are dumped on the floor. They continue on into the laundry room and bathroom where they pour laundry detergent on the floor and walls. The bedrooms are next and they completely ransack them. On the way out of the bedroom they pass the utility room where they find a gallon of white paint. They open the paint, take brushes and begin to redecorate the house. Tables, walls, floors and windows are painted. They even gave the television screen a coat of paint. After having enough fun they leave the residence through the front door. A neighbor observed that the front door was open and called the police. The responding officer entered the house and searched it for actors. He then called for the crime scene unit. They followed their routine of photographs, fingerprinting and evidence collection. They did recover fingerprints however our actors are juveniles and don't have any fingerprints on file. They did get lucky though. It seems that our actors were so focused on their destructive free for all that when they left they forgot to take their jackets. Both of the jackets contained the boy's names and addresses. Glade we didn't lose our jackets at school. When the boy's parents were confronted they denied that it was their sons who did this. It had to be somebody else. When told about the jackets, the parents said that the police planted them there.

While I'm on the subject of juveniles this story is almost unbelievable. On a warm Wednesday in June a mother talks to her 14 year old twin daughters. She explains that their father, a construction worker just got laid off from work and they didn't have enough money to pay the mortgage. If they couldn't come up with the mortgage money they would be thrown out into the street with no place to go. The state would take them and put them in foster homes and they might never see their mom and dad again. The girls started to cry. Mom told them that there was a way to get the money but the girls would have to help. The two girls said that they would do whatever they could to help so they could stay together. This was moms plan. She would take the two girls to the bank at the shopping center. She gave each of the girls a black plastic toy pistol. She also gave each of the girls a ski mask and dressed them in jeans, sneakers and black tee shirts. She gave one of the girls a note for the teller. She took them to the bank, dressed the girls up, gave them the guns and sent them into the bank with instructions to give the note to a teller. She also gave them a paper bag to give to the teller for the money. She told them that after they got the money to leave the bank, run across the parking lot to where she was waiting with the car. The two girls went into the bank guns in hand. One of them walked up to a teller and gave her the note and the bag. The teller quickly filled the bag and gave it back to the girl. The girls immediately left the bank and ran across the parking lot to mom's car and the trio left. There were three other patrons in the bank at the time of the robbery. When the girls left one of the bank employees ran out a rear door and followed the girls across the parking lot. He saw them get into the car. He saw the license plate and wrote down the number. The police arrived and were given the license plate number. The police went to home where they found the two 14 year old girls. They also found the ski masks and toy guns. They asked the girls where their mom and dad were. They said that they just left and took the money to pay the mortgage so they could save the house. They didn't know where they went to pay the mortgage. The police took the two girls into custody and went looking for mom and dad. The girl's parents were found about 9 hours later in Atlantic City, N.J. in one of the casinos. They were trying to double the money so they had money to get them through the husband's jobless period. The girls got just under $6000.00 from the bank. The house was not in any jeopardy from loss. The girls were very lucky that they weren't shot or killed while they had the plastic guns. The parents were charged with conspiracy to commit armed robbery, possession of stolen property, child endangerment and adding to the delinquency of minors. They both received 5 to 10 years. The girls were given four years' probation for armed robbery.

This next case is a burglary with surprises. In a quiet neighborhood an elderly women lived alone in a waterfront home. Her children would visit regularly. On one of these visits her son went to the residence to visit his mother only to find that she wasn't there. He looked all over the house and asked the neighbors on both side of her that she was friends with if she was there or if they had seen her. They both said no and that they hadn't seen her in two days. The son checked the mail box and noticed that there were two days of mail in the box. On his way back into the house he noticed that the bedroom window was broken and opened. He looked around the inside of the house again and saw that some drawers were ajar and the closet doors were open. Something his mother never did. He became concerned and called the police. The police arrived and made out a burglary and missing persons report. The main concern was the missing women. Behind the home was a 100 foot wide, 10 foot deep lagoon. The officer called in the crime scene unit and a search and rescue team which included divers. The crime scene unit arrived and the detective began processing the scene. A short time later the search team and divers arrived. The searches went door to door to residences around the neighborhood to ask the residents if anyone had seen the missing women. The divers went into the water and began an underwater search for the missing woman. During the processing of the burglary scene the crime scene detective notices that there is no toilet seat on the toilet in the bathroom. He takes some photographs and goes outside to his crime scene vehicle to get some more film for his camera. He notices that it is trash collection day. He glances around the street at the trash at the curbs outside the homes. He sees a couple of houses away and across the street what appears to be a toilet seat that has been put out to trash. He notifies a scene supervisor of his finding. The supervisor and another detective walked down to the trash pile to see that it is in fact a toilet seat. They went to the door of the residence and knock on the door. A young man in his early twenties answers the door. He sees the police and said what do you want, I didn't do anything. Needless to say just his statement got their interest. They interview him and come to find out that he had just been released from prison 5 days before. He was doing time for assault. When asked about the toilet seat in the trash he said that it was broken and that his roommate got a new one to replace it. The officers asked to see the new seat and he directed them to the bathroom. They went to the bathroom and looked at the seat. It clearly wasn't a new seat. Further interrogation of the man led the officers to want to question the man's roommate. The man they were speaking to had only been living there three days. The woman had been missing 4 days. The man gives them the location where his roommate works and the take the man into custody for further questioning. They then respond to the roommate's job. They approach the man and speak to him. His answers are vague and evasive. They feel that they have enough reason to take him into custody and bring him to headquarters where he is interrogated. During the interrogation process he confesses to the crime.

The actor tells the police that his intent was to burglarize the women's home. He hadn't seen her around so he thought she was with one of her children. He said he forced open the bedroom window and entered. He was looking for anything that was of value that he could sell. He also said that he took the toilet seat because his was broken. He said that he was just getting to leave when the women come walking out of the other bedroom. She started to scream so he said he hit her knocking her down. On the way down to the floor the woman's side struck the arm of the sofa which was wood. When she landed on the floor she wasn't moving. He said that he panicked because he had killed her. His only thought was to get rid of the body. He said that he went back home and got his car. He backed it into the driveway. He then picked up the women and placed her into the truck of the vehicle. He then drove about 10 miles out of town to a wooded area. He pulled the car off to the side of the road got out of the car and went to the trunk. He didn't see anyone around so he opened the trunk to get her out. This was the second time that the women would surprise him. She wasn't dead she passed out when she struck her ribs on the arm of the sofa. She grabs for his neck but he overwhelms her and strangles her until she dies. He picks her up and carries her about 200 feet from the road and leaves her body in the woods. He went on to tell us that he didn't tell his roommate what he had done. He figured if he just kept it to himself nobody would ever know. After the interview the actor agreed to take us to the spot in the woods where he disposed of the body. There was one problem. When he dumped off the body the ground was clear. When he took us to the place where the body was and there was 17 inches of new snow. The actor took us to where he thought the body was but with the snow on the ground he wasn't sure. A search of the area was made and we found a small piece of cloth at the base of a tree. There were some small animal tracks also around the cloth. We followed the animal tracks back to 2 feet from where the actor was standing with the two detectives and uncovered the woman's body from under the snow. The autopsy confirmed the actor's story. The woman had 4 broken ribs on her right side and her neck was broken from strangulation. The actor pled guilty to homicide and received a 30 year to life sentence. He would not be eligible for parole for 30 years. The roommate was released.

The case that I am going to discuss now is one of the most difficult I've ever had to investigate. As a crime scene investigator you always get to see the aftermath of what has happened never the actual act. In this case the victim is a woman in her 30's owns a store where she collects items from yard and garage sales. She then sells these items for a profit. Unlike a pawn shop she doesn't accept items on consignment. She would buy them and then resell them. The time of day is 7:30 pm. The store closes at 7:00 pm. A passing patrol car sees that the store is still open and stops to see if anything is wrong. The officer enters the store and sees the victim's lifeless body lying face down on the floor. She appears to have been stabbed multiple times and is covered in blood. He returns to his patrol car and calls headquarters. The officer secures the crime and waits for the crime scene unit to arrive. When we arrived we examined the scene and noticed that several areas in the rear of the store were in disarray. There also was a large amount of blood spattering around the shop. The cash register was opened and empty. The store also had video surveillance cameras but there wasn't a recording tape in the VCR. We proceeded to process the scene looking for clues. There were many fingerprints but then again it was a shop open to the public. The items in the shop were the type of things that people would pick up and examine before they bought them. Many items had to be taken to the crime lab for processing including over 1000 music compact disc. The scene took two days to process and when we were done we were no closer to making an arrest or solving the crime then we were when we started. We were processing the items collected at the scene when we were advised that bloody clothing was found in a dumpster. We responded to the dumpster location and were met by a patrol officer and a homeless man. The homeless man was searching through the dumpster looking for aluminum cans he could take to the recycling yard and redeem for cash. In the process he found bloody clothing and called the police thinking that there was a body in the dumpster and that he would get a reward for finding it. We searched the dumpster and found shoes, pants and a shirt all with heavy blood staining. We also found a VCR tape. The items were taken into evidence and brought back to the crime lab for processing. The detectives also gave the homeless man $20.00 and took him to a local diner and fed him.

The items collected from the dumpster were given priority and were processed immediately. The blood on the clothing belonged to our victim. We put the video tape in our VCR player and began watching the tape. The tape was over seven hours long. To our amazement it was a video recording of the actual homicide. We started to view the last half hour of the tape first. That's where we say the actor kill the victim. By watching the events unfold we learned that the actor was in the store over two hours waiting for the store to close. As the victim began closing he attacked her with a knife. The autopsy revealed that the victim had been stabbed 37 times. The actor was chasing her around the shop stabbing her as she ran. That explained the blood spattering all over the store. He finally caught up to her in the rear of the store where they wrestled and knocked shelving over. She broke loose and he caught her again in the spot where her body was found. He continued to stab her and then stood back to watch her die. Every moment was recorded on tape. We were able to count each of the stab wounds as they were administered. We actually saw her exact moment of death. This was one of the hardest things I've ever had to watch. You wanted to reach out to help her but you couldn't. We still didn't know who the actor was but after developing his fingerprints on the VCR tape case we went to make an arrest. He wasn't at his residence when we got there so we left. We told neighbors to call us if he returned. We received a telephone call from suspect wanting to know what we wanted. We had a warrant for the suspect for auto theft and told him it was in reference to that. He said that he didn't steal the car but knew who did. We agreed to meet him at a local shopping mall in exchange for the information and told him that if he didn't steal the car that we would let him go. He agreed and we arrested him on site. After several hours of interrogation he confessed to the homicide and the auto theft. He said that he had wanted to buy something from the store two days before the homicide and had an argument with the victim over the price and went back to steal it that day he murdered her. He was sentenced life in prison.

CHAPTER SEVEN

The Long Arm Of The Law

The cases in this chapter relate to almost getting away with murder. The first case I will be discussing circumstantial evidence. If you remember when we discussed evidence in the beginning we covered circumstantial evidence. To refresh your memory there were three types of evidence, Real, Direct and Circumstantial. Circumstantial evidence is the evidence that tends to prove the facts at hand by inference. It doesn't really come right out and say it. It only infers to the facts.

This is a case where a 17 year old high school girl is infatuated with the charms of a 20 year old man. They have been carrying on a relationship for quite a while. She was still in high school and he was already graduated. She would see him every day after school or on some days just cut school completely. It came to be that one day she didn't come home from school. It was a Friday and although she would sometimes come home late she would call home to let her family know that she was ok. On this particular Friday she did not come home and she didn't call. Her parents tried making calls to her friends with no success. They had a good idea where she was. They didn't like her with this boy but knew that she was seeing him against their wishes. They tried to stop her from seeing him but knew they couldn't. When she didn't come home by Saturday morning they began to worry. They knew where this boy lived and went to his house but his mother said that he hadn't been home in a couple of days which wasn't unusual for him. Not having any success they tried calling her friends again to see if anyone had heard from her but they said no. They were now desperate and worried so they called the police. The police came and filed a missing persons report on the girl. They also described the boy in the report. Detectives started an investigation and interviewed as many of her friends as they could find. During these interviews they spoke to one of the missing girls girlfriends. She said that she had confided in her that she was going to break off the relationship that she had with the boy. She said that he had gotten weird and she no longer wanted to be with him. She was going to tell him on Friday when she met him after school. The detectives then went and interviewed the boy's mother. She told them that he had moved out of the house 2 weeks before. She said that she didn't know exactly where he was only that he was living in a motel in a beach community not far away. He hadn't called her and she didn't know which town or which motel. The detectives notified all the beach communities in the area and handed out fliers with the girls and boys pictures on it. It didn't take long detectives were going to businesses in the beach towns and handing out the fliers. They entered a convenience store in this one town and handed the clerk the flier. He looked at the flier and said yes that he knew the boy and in fact he was just in the store about an hour before. They asked if the girl was with him and he said no. He said he has never seen the girl. They asked the clerk if he knew where the boy lived. He said that he thought that he lived somewhere nearby. The detectives told him to call them if he came back and left. They called for additional officers to help the search all the local motels for the boy. In a small motel about a block away from the convenience store where the clerk identified him the motel manager identified him as living there about two weeks. He also said that he did see a girl matching the girl's picture with him once. The motel was a four room complex. His room was the second unit in from the corner. They knocked on the door and didn't get an answer. They got the motel manager to open the door. They looked inside and called out his name but didn't get an answer. They had a patrol car sit out front of the room while they went for a search warrant. Other detective units were parked around the area in case he showed up. The two investigating detectives returned with the warrant and entered the motel room. The room was bare. There was no carpeting on the floor, it had been removed. It was cut away from the edges of the wall. Other than a black plastic bag on the bed and 7 items hanging in the closet, the room was empty. In the bathroom was one tooth brush, tooth paste, a throw away razor and a can of shaving cream. The detectives searched the rooms thoroughly. In the bathroom under the sink they found four school books belonging to the missing girl. The called the crime lab to have some Luminol delivered. They darkened the room and applied the Luminol. There were some minor reactions on the back of the door but one reaction gave them some hope. On a shirt hanging in the closet they found a small red stain. They collected the stain and sent it to the lab for DNA matching. As they were getting ready to leave they received a call from one of the surveillance teams that they had the boy in custody. They brought him back to the motel. The two detectives asked him where he was and he said walking. They asked him where the girl was and he said what girl. They said your girlfriend. He said that she wasn't his girlfriend anymore they broke up. They asked when and he said two weeks ago. They said if you broke up two weeks ago why you broke up two weeks ago why are her school books under the sink in the bathroom? He said oh she left them in my car and I was going to give them back to her. They asked him what happened to the carpet from the motel room. He said that there wasn't any carpet there when he moved in. One of the detectives went to the manager and showed him the floors apartment and asked him about the carpet. He said its on the floor. The detective brought him to the room and showed him the floor. He became quite upset that the carpet was missing. He said he just had it installed a year ago. They let the manager go back to his apartment. They asked the boy again about the carpet and he said that it wasn't there when he moved in. They asked him where his car was and he said around the rear of the motel complex. They went around the rear of the building to his car and searched it. It turned out that the car wasn't his, it was his mother's. He borrowed it from her. Neither the boy nor his mother mentioned that. They didn't find anything. They had the car impounded and taken to the lab. While looking around the car a detective found a blood stained crowbar on the ground about 6 feet from the car in some deep grass. The crowbar was also sent to the lab. When they completed the scene they took the boy back to headquarters for further questioning.

While they were questioning the boy again the lab results were given to the detectives. The blood stain from the shirt was the girls as was the blood on the crowbar. In the trunk of the car there was a reaction to a Luminol test and the blood found in the trunk was the girls. In addition to the blood found in the trunk carpet fibers were found that match the carpet fibers in the motel room. Once again they asked him about the carpet and again he said it wasn't there when he rented the room. They then charged the boy with hindering an investigation and locked him up.

The detectives being at a loss were looking through the boy's belongings. They found a credit card receipt for gas from a gas station in Long Island NY. The gas station was about 100 miles away from the motel. They ran a credit card check on the rest of his credit cards and found that he also purchased food in a restaurant in the same town. The bill was for $57.00. They asked the boy about these charges and he denied having knowledge of any of it.

Not getting anywhere with the boy they decided to go to Long Island NY. They talked to people in the restaurant and the gas station. The gas station attendant remembered him. He said that he had asked directions. He didn't remember where. He did say that he parked over by the trash dumpster and it looked like he was cleaning out trash from his car. They asked when the trash was picked up and the attendant said the same day that the boy was there a couple of hours after he left. They took the name off of the dumpster and called the carting company. They told them the date and time that the dumpster was emptied and which land fill it was emptied in. It took until the next day when they could organize a search party. The searchers went to the land fill and with the assistance of heavy equipment began excavating the land fill in search of the carpet. After two days of searching they found nothing. The detectives built a circumstantial evidence case and presented it to the grand jury. They felt that there was enough evidence to take the case to trial. At the trial all the evidence was presented. The jury felt that the victim lied when making his statements. Specifically those pertaining to the school books, carpet and going to Long Island, NY. They also felt that there was enough evidence to support the fact the girl was in the motel room and in the trunk of the car. There was evidence to support that the girl had been beaten with the crowbar. There was also sufficient evidence to show that the girl was taken to a dumpster in Long Island, NY in the carpet and dumped there. It took the jury 4 hours to return a guilty verdict. He was sentenced to life in prison with no eligibility of parole for 30 years. What makes this case hard is that we had to get a conviction without the body of the victim. I felt good about the conviction however and I feel that there is more to this case. I really don't think he acted alone but I guess that's a crime for another day.

This next case is also a case built on circumstantial evidence. This case was the first major homicide case that I had been assigned to. I actually was handed this case by default. I had only been in the unit 6 months and was still pretty green when it came to crime scene processing. It was about 1:00 pm and I was assigned to cover the front desk and the telephones while the secretary was at lunch. The other the detectives were either out processing other crime scenes, in court or out to lunch. The only other person in the office was the Lieutenant in charge of the unit. The telephone rang and I answered it. On the other end of the phone was a police dispatcher from a local town who was excited saying send the crime scene unit we have a murdered woman and there is blood all over. She finally got around to giving me the address. I went to notify the Lieutenant to see which detectives he wanted to give the call to. He was on his way out the door to lunch when I found him. He said who's here. I responded that it was just me. He told me to get to the scene and gather all the information I could from the local police and then start taking exterior overall photographs only. I responded as ordered. A short time later other officers started to respond to assist. The first officer to respond is usually given the case but seeing as I was still new it went to the second officer who responded. I gave him the information that I had collected and went on about my assignment. About an hour had passed when the Lieutenant approached me and asked if I was done and I said yes. He said great because the other detective's camera broke and he was unable to photograph the scene. It was now my job. He said take your time and don't miss anything. I believe I took over 700 photographs that day. From there it was you who already started the case you might as well finish it.

The victim a 68 year old woman ran a rooming house in the town. The way the house was set up was simple. The home was originally built as a two family home, one family upstairs and one family down stairs. The upstairs home was broken into three separate bedrooms which shared a common bathroom and kitchen. There was a common entrance stairway and all the rooms shared a common hallway. The victim lived downstairs by herself. There never seemed to be any problems at the house. In fact the house was a gathering place for people around the neighborhood. The information given me by the responding officers was that the victim ran a high stakes poker game on Thursdays. It was called a skins game. Locals would come by and gamble. The victim controlled the bank. She would go to the bank on Thursday afternoon and withdraw cash to bank the game Thursday evening. Apparently someone else had other ideas.

I entered the scene to take an overall look at what we were dealing with. I was directed to the master bedroom which was off the kitchen. The room looked as though someone had searched it. Drawers and closets were open and things were pulled out of them. The bed was made but had some blood splatter on it. There also were some tissues on the bed. The television was on and there were lottery tickets on top of it. The victim was lying on the floor on the far side of the bed in front of the window. She was wearing a maroon camisole nothing else. There was blood all over. In fact this was the bloodiest scene I had ever seen. It was actually the bloodiest scene I ever saw right up to the day I retired. I made sure that everyone was out of the house to keep the scene secured. When my Lieutenant arrived he was as stunned as I was. He looked at me and asked me if I wanted to give this case to a more experienced detective or did I think that I could handle it, I said I could and he said if you need assistance ask. It's your case, your call. You make the assignments. It was like jumping into the deep end when you just learned how to swim. We proceed to process the scene with photographs, video and searching for evidence. The medical examiner arrived and we examined the victim's body. She was lying on her back. She had been stabbed several times. In addition her throat was slashed from ear to ear down to the neck bone. Not once but twice. She also had one of her fingernails stuck in her side. It broke off during an apparent struggle. The autopsy would later tell us that she had been stabbed a total of 16 times in addition to the trauma to her neck. She also had several defense wounds on her hands and fingers. The wounds were made with an extremely sharp implement and were teardrop in shape. Looking at the wounds and taking into account the sharpness of the blade indicated to me that it was a straight razor. The victim's body was prepared and bagged and sealed. She was taken to the morgue. We collected the evidence we found. Most of it was blood samples, the lottery tickets and a few miscellaneous items from around the room. There were two facial tissues on the bed that had very faint blood stains on them so we took them as well. Remember these. Once the victim's body was removed we continued processing the scene looking for clues. We started interviewing the neighbors and the residents that were home living upstairs. We didn't have much to go on at this point so we resorted to Luminol. This was my first experience using the Luminol so I was a little unsure about it. My main concern was that I was told that we needed to use respirators because the fumes were toxic. We started the Luminol examination as soon as it had become dark. We went into the bedroom where the victim was found and started spraying the Luminol where her body was. As you might expect the blood all illuminated. There was one surprise however, there was a footwear mark in blood starting at the victim's body and leading out to the kitchen. It was a left footwear mark.

We followed the footwear marks out to the kitchen, down the hall and out onto the porch. The marks continued into the entrance to the upstairs and up the stairs. We saw two marks on the stairs themselves. They continued again at the top of the stairs and down a short hallway to the door of the one resident who wasn't home as yet. The resident arrived home later that evening. We were still working on the scene. As a matter of fact I worked on the scene 7 straight days. We confronted the resident and asked him where he was all day. He said that he was at work. The one thing we noticed was that he had a bandage on one of his fingers. He said that he cut his finger at work. He said his girlfriend bandaged it for him with duct tape but he put the bandage on it. We asked permission to search his room and he told us to get a warrant and we did. Inside his room there were some tiny blood drops on the door and a speck of blood on a sweatshirt in his closet. He said that they were his from when he was changing the duct tape. There was a roll of duct tape in his room. We inquired at his job if he had been cut but were told the workers get cuts there all the time and usually don't report them. We spoke to his girlfriend and she said that she did assist him with the cut. One of the other residents of the house told me that a while back the victim and our suspect were sort of boyfriend and girlfriend but that it was now over. Finally we flat out asked him if he murdered the women. Without hesitation he said "If you think I killed her, prove it!" We took all our evidence back to the lab for processing. You have to understand a couple of things at this point. First, this case happened in 1989. DNA testing in 1989 required a large amount of blood in order to perform a test. Second, although the blood led a trail into his room it only proved that whoever was in the room standing next to the victim in the blood walked from the bedroom, through the house, up the stairs and went into the suspect's room. It doesn't necessarily mean that it was the suspect. He still remains a suspect. The case remained open for many years. From time to time I would reopen it and see if there was something we missed. It wasn't until 2005 that we decided to re-examine all the blood evidence with the new DNA procedures and see if we could find any definite proof. The new DNA results did help telling us that the blood speck on the sweatshirt in his closet was from the victim. It still wasn't enough to get a conviction. We talked and decided to try to get a DNA match on the two tissues with the faint blood stains that we found on the bed. We still didn't know if we had enough blood but we were willing to give it a try. When we received the results we still didn't know if we had enough to get a conviction. The results was one of the tissues was a positive from the victim. I need to explain DNA results. The results are administered in numbers of possible conclusion. The results say that the probability of this being positive is so many millions or billions to 1. With the second tissue the results were positive with the probability being 39,000 to one being the suspect. By DNA standards this is not a sure thing. There is one other fact in the test that gave us what we thought would be enough to go to trial and get a conviction. The blood sample had a specific blood trait not all that common. It's called Sickle Cell. The blood sample had it and the suspect had it. That gave us what we needed. It took 16 years but now we were ready to try the case. The entire time we kept track of the suspect's whereabouts which was presently in Virginia. Some other background information that came out while investigating all those years was that the suspect was exiled from Trinidad for two homicides. Finally the day came and they went to arrest the suspect. They introduced themselves to him and asked him if he knew who they were? He said yes, they were the same detectives who questioned him in 1989. They told him that back in 1989 you made a statement where you said "If you think I killed her, prove it!" Well we proved it and your under arrest for homicide. He was taken into custody and returned to this jurisdiction for trial.

At trial I was called upon to testify as were all the other people still working that hadn't retired. The defense put up a good fight but the prosecutor presented his case perfectly. The circumstantial evidence was strong. The defense tried to discredit everyone to no avail. The defendant never showed an emotion or said a word. He didn't take the stand in his own defense. It took the jury a day and a half but came back with a guilty plea. He was sentenced to life with no parole eligibility for 30 years. When the verdict was read and at the sentencing he never so much as blinked an eye. The crime was a cold blooded murder. The murderer was a cold blood killer.

There are times during the processing of a crime scene investigation that certain information is withheld from the press and everyone not directly involved in the case. Sometimes in tough cases we withhold information that only the killer would know. This is information from the scene in which you would have had to been there to know.

This next case starts in one state and is solved in another. Our actor is driving home late one Saturday evening from the Jersey shore to Staten Island, NY. He leaves the resort town and is hungry. He gets about 5 miles out of town while driving on a state highway when he sees a local pizza restaurant. He pulls in and goes inside for a slice of pizza. There isn't anybody in the store except the man making the pizza. He orders the pizza and soft drink. He sits down at a table and waits for his order. When his order is ready it is brought to him. He eats the pizza and has a conversation with the store owner. They talk about business, the weather and the town. The actor finishes the pizza and asks the owner for another slice telling him how good it was. The owner walks behind the counter to heat up another slice. He puts it in the oven to warm just as the telephone rings. He's talking on the telephone to a business partner and tells him what a good day it has been. He said that he had several large orders and it was the best night he had all week. He hangs up the telephone and brings our actor his second slice of pizza. He then returns to the counter and begins folding pizza boxes. He leaves the counter and goes into the back room to get more boxes. When he returns the actor is standing behind the counter by the cash register. The owner says what do you think you're doing? The actor says robbing you and strikes the owner with the pizza paddle and knocks him to the floor. The owner tries to get up but the actor punches him and knocks him unconscious. He then grabs a roll of duct tape from under the counter and binds the owner's hand and feet. He also tapes his mouth closed. He empties the register which only has about $100.00 in it. He looks around under the counter and sees a shoebox under a receipt book. He opens it and finds almost $2000.00 in cash along with some checks. He takes the cash and leaves the checks. Realizing that the owner can identify him he takes a knife from the counter and stabs the owner one time in the chest killing him. He leaves the restaurant and drives on to Staten Island, NY. Shortly afterwards another patron comes in and finds the murdered owner on the floor and calls police. The crime scene unit is called and starts to process the scene. From an evidence stand point we didn't have much. Our best piece of evidence is the duct tape used on the victim. The victim is taken for an autopsy and the duct tape is removed and sent to the crime lab. The duct tape is stuck together and has to be separated to be able to recover fingerprints from the sticky side of the tape. This must be done in a certain manner so as not to distort the prints while separating the tape. The process we use to separate the tape is simple. We freeze it and then just snap the pieces apart. Then it is placed in a solution called Crystal Violet. It's a deep purple liquid and sticks to the prints on the sticky side of the tape. After processing the tape we only recovered partial fingerprints on the tape. No evidence, no witnesses, the case went cold.

About 2 years later we receive a call from a man in Staten Island, NY who tells us that he overheard a conversation in a bar between two men when one of them mentioned that he was coming home from the Jersey shore one Saturday night and killed a guy in a pizza place. We sent two detectives to Staten Island and met with the man. He told them he sitting in a booth having a beer and a sandwich when he heard the conversation of two men in the booth next to him. One man said that he killed a man in a pizza restaurant on his way home from the Jersey shore. He said he beat the man, duct taped his hands, feet and mouth and then stabbed him in the chest. They knew that one of the men in the booth was the killer. During the investigation nothing was ever said about duct tape but he knew about the duct tape. They asked the informer if he knew the man and he said no but he does frequent the bar often. He gave them a description and they staked out the bar. Four days later the man walked into the bar and was detained until the informer could be brought over to confirm that they had the right man. The informer confirmed that they had the same man who was talking in the bar to another man. The man was returned for trial where he received 30years to life for homicide with no parole eligibility for 30 years. He also got a 10 year sentence for strong arm robbery to be run consecutively with the homicide sentence. That's a 40 year sentence for $2000.00, 2 slices of pizza and a soft drink.

It was a nice day and a gentleman living in a retirement community decided to take his dog for a walk. He and the dog would go for a walk almost every day. They would go to an area by a well-traveled road that was at the west end of the community. Alongside this road was a dirt road that went off into the woods. This dirt road was also used regularly. He would take his dog to this area because he could unleash the dog and let him run. The dog would get his exercise and the owner knew that he would be safe from traffic. On this particular day he called the dog to come back and he didn't. He called again and again. Finally the dog came back. It seemed that he found something in the trash. This area was also was a dumping area for construction debris. As the dog approached he owner couldn't believe his eyes. The dog was carrying what looked like a human arm and hand. When the dog got closer he realized that it was in fact a human arm and hand. He put the dog on its leash and went to the road and flagged down a motorist. They called the police to the scene. The police arrived and walked down the dirt road looking at several piles of trash they were passing along the way. About 100 yards down the road they came to a pile of trash. It had several plastic trash bags lying on the ground, one of which was torn open. They examined one of the other bags and observed what appeared to be a human leg inside. They called the crime scene unit and secured the area awaiting their arrival. The crime scene unit took an overall look at what was there and then began to process the crime scene. They followed their procedures and took photographs and made a video recording of everything at that scene. They began searching the bags. There were seven bags. One was empty it was the one that was torn open. It was the one that contained the arm and hand that the dog had brought to his owner. In the other six bags were the other arm and hand, an upper torso and a lower torso, two legs and foot combinations and a head. The remarkable thing was that none of the bags had any significant amounts of blood in them. It would be found out later at the autopsy that the bones appeared to be precision cut with a saw. They were cut clean enough to have been surgically cut. This indicated that the victim was killed somewhere else and then dumped here in the woods. Another common thing of all the bags was that each body part was triple bagged in plastic bags. The exterior bag was black and the interior bags were white with a logo on them. All black bags were the same and all the white bags were the same.

The body parts were void of clothing. There wasn't anything identifiable on the victim except a tattoo on one of legs that said "Fast Eddie". The remains were taken to the morgue where they were examined with the results that I stated before. The hands were fingerprinted and we got a positive result and identified the victim. Running the background on the victim found that the victim had prior arrest most of which were minor offenses. He was also known to be a homosexual. That was about the extent as this case could go at this time. The processing of the bags for fingerprints was positive. We recovered a couple of fingerprints that were good enough for comparison. They were run through local and national AFIS systems but no positive results were received. This means that the person leaving these fingerprints is not on file. He or she has never been fingerprinted. The unknown fingerprints are also kept in a database and periodically rerun against the files to see if the person has been fingerprinted and see if we can get a match. A match in law enforcement language is called a hit.

Before I continue let me explain what AFIS is. AFIS is an acronym for Automated Fingerprint Identification System. This system maintains fingerprint cards on file for the purpose of comparing unknown fingerprints to see if they can be identified. Every state in the United States has this system as well as the federal government. The system is also being used internationally as well. Having no clues other than knowing who our victim is we hit a dead end. A fifty state bulletin was released to all law enforcement agencies containing information about the case and the victim. As it turns out we immediately receive three responses to our bulletin. All have

89

the same types of case that we do right down to the plastic bags and victim's condition. Only one of the other cases recovered a fingerprint of good value for comparison. They also ran it through the AFIS with negative results. We checked their fingerprint against ours but they didn't match. That's not to say that it's not the same killer just from a different finger. More similar facts are that all the victims are males and all are homosexual. All were dismembered into seven parts, bled out before they were bagged in triple bags. What two words do you think came to mind instantly, right Serial Killer. The challenge was on. All the agencies kept in close contact and shared all the evidence results they had. It was about 3 months since our victim was found when we received a telephone call that two human legs with feet attached were found in a trash barrel in a rest area along a major roadway. We responded to the scene and recovered the legs. They were removed the same way with the same saw marks and triple bagged the same way. A couple of days later the other five parts were recovered in an adjoining state. We knew that we had at least five victims at this point and could make a good argument for six more bring our total to eleven. The question was what did these five victims have in common? We knew for a fact that they were all males and they were all homosexuals. Everyone's investigation led to one place. All the victims patronized a gay bar in New York City. All the victims were last seen in that bar. Here's the best one, all the bodies were dumped 100 miles from the bar in various directions. Not all in the same place but all 100 miles away from the bar. Detectives investigated the bar but nobody remembers any one person being with the victims. They remember the victims but not one common person with all of them. Once again we reach a dead end until six years later when a police officer makes a motor vehicle stop. The driver is questioned and taken into custody for minor offenses. As part of the arrest procedures the driver is fingerprinted and a mug shot taken during the booking process. Like I mentioned before AFIS keeps all fingerprints on record and periodically the unknown files are run against the fingerprint card database. That was done in this case and when the drivers fingerprints were run against the file a positive hit came up. The only problem was that the driver had been released days before because the search or re-launch wasn't done until after he was released. The information from the arrest was on file and the name and address of the suspect was known. Detectives responded to the suspect's residence and he was arrested and taken into custody. The five murders that we knew of for sure were in various jurisdictions and questions were raised who would do the prosecution? Seeing as how New Jersey had the only cases that yielded fingerprints New Jersey was given the task. At the time of trial the suspect was charged with two homicides and fingerprint experts tied the victim to both cases. Additionally he was tied to the plastic bags, the bar and trips to and from the dump locations by credit card receipts for gas and food to and from the dumping sites. He was found guilty on both murders and was sentenced to two life sentences to run consecutively with no eligibility of parole for 30 years on each case. That relates to no chance of parole for 60 years. The other cases are pending and other cases are being brought out as time goes by. How many is he really responsible for?

CHAPTER EIGHT

It's All About Turf

I know that every time we pick up a newspaper, turn on the radio or television the news usually has some items about gangs or gang related activity. The major gang problem in this country started on the west coast. It was originally started to protect groups of people in the neighborhood from persecution from outsiders. They formed in the neighborhoods for the neighborhoods to protect the neighborhoods. Well that mushroomed into what we have today. Today's gangs protect their turf. The turf is where they conduct their business. That business may be illegal drugs, prostitution and sales of illegal guns. There are probably several other businesses they operate but the point here is their turf, their home areas. It has to do a lot with gang affiliations and command structure. Don't say that you're a gang member if you're not. That could be dangerous at the very least. The gangs identify themselves by the color of clothes they wear along with gang tattoos. Each gang has its own symbols, hand signs and rules. The basic rule is to do whatever the gang tells you to do. The more orders you follow whether selling drugs, shooting someone, stealing something etc. the higher in rank you can achieve. I will keep using the word gangs instead of using the gang names. I don't feel we should glorify their names they don't rate it. If they did well I'd be the first to give them name credit.

This first case is one of someone saying he was something that he wasn't, a high ranking gang member. The fact of this story is not only was he not a high ranking gang member but he wasn't a member of a gang at all. His thing was that he was selling something on the gang's turf. We weren't sure but we assumed that it was drugs although no drugs were found at the scene at the time. The only thing we found was several copies of the same music CD. Our story starts in an apartment complex where we have had gang related problems for years. Our victim is attempting to sell we think drugs to three young males. He tells them that he is a General in the local gang. They are impressed being young and wanting to be gang members themselves one day. They buy his goods and move on. They next encounter one of the real gang members. He asks them what they are doing. They tell them of their purchase from the General around the corner. He says what General? They describe the man to the gang member and he goes around the corner. Normally that would be it but it's not. The gang member confronts the so called General and tells him to leave the area or there would be a price to pay. The General says I'm not paying anybody especially you. The gang member laughs and walks off. It only took about 20 minutes before the gang member returned with two other gang members. The so called General now a scared private takes off running across the parking lot as shots are being fired. He jumps a fence into the back yard of a home along the parking lot. The three gang members follow him over the fence and into the back yard. They separate to go around the house. Two of the gang members follow the impostor around the house while the other gang member goes around the other side of the house. They all meet up in the front of the house where the man claiming to be a gang member is gunned down on the front lawn of the home. That's where he is left and found when the police arrive. The gang members left and no arrest have been made and the turf is one impostor less.

This case is drug related. In a local town a man goes to visit his mother and brother. He knocks on the door and nobody answers. He goes around the rear of the house and finds that the kitchen sliding door is open. The home is in disarray. He calls out to his mother but she doesn't answer. He calls out to his brother but he doesn't answer either. He starts looking around for them and goes upstairs. He goes into the bedroom and finds his mother and brother dead on the bed and bloody. He picked up the telephone and calls the police. The police arrive, view the scene and remove the son from the house. Crime scene was called. When crime scene arrived they immediately made an immediate overall examination, the home was in disarray and had apparently been searched. Everything is open and items were removed from them and thrown on the floor. In the bed the two victims were lying on the bed. They had their hands and feet bound and they were gaged. They had been shot. There was a pillow that was next to the bodies that had burn marks and blood stains on it. It appeared that the pillow was used to muffle the sound of the gunshots. The victims were shot gangland style. During interviews of residence in the neighborhood it was found that people would come and go to and from the residence 24 hours a day. It was a house where known drug dealers and users would be known to frequent. Our investigation developed leads to drug connections in New York City. According to relatives several items were taken from the victims such as jewelry. We felt that robbery wasn't the intent of this double homicide but actors were certainly looking for something.

We processed the crime scene collecting a lot of evidence and doing some extensive fingerprinting. We also made an extensive search of the residence. During that search one of the detectives was coming down the stairs from the second floor when he noticed a large bag of drugs on the top of the kitchen hutch. Another detective found a very large bag of drugs hidden under the steps that led from the back yard to the sliding glass doors into the kitchen. This was obviously what the actors were looking for.

I mentioned before that jewelry was taken from one of the victims. A ring that one of the victims wore all the time turned up in New York City. An investigation in New York City developed a suspect with knowledge of the double homicide. We dispatched two of our detectives to New York City and worked jointly with the police there. That proved to be the breaking point in the case. Suspects were developed and the story unfolded. It was a drug related homicide. The drugs that were being searched for were bought from a different distributor then the ones previously used. That made one gangs turf cross another gang's turf. The actors were caught, tried and sentenced.

It seemed like a simple thing to do, go and get a haircut. You would think it was simple and you never would have the slightest thought that it would kill you. Our victim is a local man in town. He has been known to deal with drugs from time to time. This particular day he was going to the barber shop to get his hair cut. It was late in the afternoon. He was called to the back of the shop when it was his turn. He took his seat and started talking to the barber and a 9 year boy who was next to him. They were all the way in the rear of the shop in the last room. Each room had a different purpose. There was a beauty salon area, a hair styling area and a hair cutting area for men. In the very rear of the store was a small shop that sold combs, brushes, hair treatments lotions and music CD. It was a very popular place in the neighborhood and usually very busy. The barber started cutting his hair and the usual barber shop conversations were being discussed, weather, health etc. About 20 minutes into the his hair cut three men wearing ski masks came in through the front door of the shop, went to the rear hair cutting room and shot the victim several times in front of several witnesses. They then ran out the rear door of the shop through the store area. The victim lay dead on the floor in a pool of blood. The nine year old boy was in shock and crying. Everyone in shop was stunned. They couldn't believe what just happened in front of them. They were all eyewitnesses to a savage murder and it happened right before their eyes. Police were called and immediately responded. They secured the scene and took all the witnesses to headquarters. The 9 year old boy was taken to the hospital where he was examined and released. The police called the crime scene unit and the swat team. The swat team was called because word on the street was that the murder was retaliation from a prior incident between the victim and the shooter and it wasn't over. There were more shootings to come.

When we arrived at the scene we were escorted by the swat team. The entire time we were processing the swat team secured the area. We entered the barber shop through the front door and took a quick overall view of what was inside. The victim was located in the rear work area lying on the blood soaked floor. He as lying on his back, next to him was a knocked over stool. There was blood splatters all over the areas around him. There appeared to be bullet holes in the wall. In the main work area outside the room where the victim was shot there were several spent shell casings. Several stools and chairs were knocked over out there as well. Witnesses said that the actors knocked them over as they ran into the barber shop.

The crime scene investigation started with video recording and photographing. The scene being as large as it was required that it be divided into sections. Two detective teams were assigned to each section of which there were 6 different areas. Due to the type of business we were in we decided not to vacuum for hair and fiber evidence. Blood samples were collected. Fingerprints were also collected from all the persons who were present at the time of the shooting. The reason for this was so that these people could be eliminated from any fingerprints that were recovered during the fingerprinting process. A very methodical search was undertaken for evidence. Spent shell casings were collected and projectiles (bullets) were recovered from the walls. During the fingerprint processing numerous fingerprints were recovered from the entrance door and counter areas. Witness statements were also taken and suspects were developed. An autopsy was performed on the victim and it was determined that his cause of death was as a result of receiving multiple gunshot wounds. The evidence was taken back to the crime lab for processing. Blood samples were tested, shell casings were processed for fingerprints and ballistic examinations were made. Days passed and investigations continued. Eventually detectives arrested three suspects and charged them with homicide. It was also determined during the investigation through the testimony of an informant that the shooting was as a result of drug dealing on the street. Drug dealers were shooting drug dealers.

A date was set for trial and it was decided to try the three defendants together rather than have three separate trials. The trial started and was what we call a high profile, high risk trial. This simply means it drew a lot of interest and a lot of threats. The threats were so intense that the prosecutors and the judge were put under 24 hour 7 day a week protection. The informant was kept in an undisclosed location for his safety. The trial proceeded and witness after witness testified. The informant testified and told his story of how the shooting was to occur and who was to be there. He named the defendant's and the victim. The forensic investigators and detectives testified as well. Somehow probably through a visit at the jail or during a telephone conversation the defendant's ordered an execution of the informant. On the day following we were called to respond to the home of the mother of the informant. In the early morning an armed assailant kicked in the door and began shooting the people inside. He only got to fire two shots before his gun jammed and he fled. One person was injured, the informants mother. The gunman ran off but was seen. Through another informer the assailant was caught and confessed. The defendants were charged with conspiracy to commit homicide and will face a second trial. The second shootings defendant and informer pled guilty and received reduced sentences. The defendant's in the barber shop shootings were all convicted of murder and sentenced to 30 years to life with no parole eligibility for 30 years. Any sentences they receive for the other charges for the attempted homicide of the witness that testified against them will most likely be added to their present sentences. These things seem to snowball into more and more after a while. I mean do they go after the new informer or confessed shooter? As they say there is no honor among criminals. Sentences are handed down day after day but the gangs go on. They go on in the streets and also in the jails. Some gangs are even controlled from the jails. It's all about turf.

Gang warfare is one of our biggest and fastest growing law enforcement problems. Gang tasks forces exist in every state in this county. Everyday law enforcement takes to the streets to do what they can. The problem is that the gangs are better armed and a lot of times better funded. Gangs get their funds from drugs, prostitution and thefts. Illegal gun sales are just as common as illegal drug sales. The more drugs the more guns. The more guns and drugs the more money. The more money the more drugs and guns. It just keeps going around and around. The other thing the gangs have is unlimited supply of people who want to be in the gang. In the gang is safety, strength and being a part of a family like atmosphere. The gangs pray on those who don't have loving caring homes. They offer those that have broken homes or come from under income families a chance to have money, status and love. I used the word love but it's the love they need. Their kind of love can end as somebody higher ups whim. It can end at the end of a barrel of a gun. It doesn't matter to the gang. They have plenty of replacements standing by to take their place. Their existence is like a cancer a plague on life. Their mere existence destroys our society. If they had their way there would only be the gang. Where they miss the point is that without our present societies to buy their drugs there would be no purpose for the gang to exist. We don't need to stop the gang so to speak but to stop and shutdown the gang's market place. If they don't have a market for their drugs and don't have a line of want to be members there is no gang. Stopping the gangs is everyone's job. Let law enforcement deal with the violence but the public has to eliminate the gangs market. How foolish would they look then? Nobody would want to be a member then. As I said one of the biggest problems we face today but not one we can't fix.

CHAPTER NINE

You Really Don't Want
To Do This

In this chapter I collected a couple of case that might have better served the actor to think twice. I will try to give you all the details and let you decide. In this first case I will set the scene. We have two middle aged gentlemen who have over acquired their taste for alcohol. These two men were drinking buddies in the fullest sense of the word. They would pan handle together, live together and of course drink together. They would pool their money together and decide which way they could get the most alcohol. On a beautiful spring day they were in of their favorite drinking spots discussing the problems of life. The area they were in was a wooded section of town. It was actually quite picturesque. There was a sizable pond along a dirt road which was covered from above by the surrounding trees. It had a large clearing at one end that overlooked the pond. It's as nice as I described it. In fact if you looking for a place to build a new home this could very well be your kind of place. Getting back to the two men, on this one afternoon they were intoxicated as usual. One of them noticed a large brown mark on his chest. He seemed very concerned and asked his friend what he thought it might be? After taking a long look his leaned back and shook his head and said I saw that once before on a guy and he died from AIDS. I think you have AIDS. The man was in shock. He said what should I do? His friend said its AIDS what can you do? He said that's terrible. Thinking for a moment he says you know if I have AIDS so do you. His buddy says how do you figure that I don't have any spots? The man says we've been drinking from the same cans and bottles for months. I might even have gotten the AIDS from you. His buddy was beside himself. You're right he says now what do we do? They drink another bottle of wine, sharing it of course, and decide that the thought of dying from AIDS was totally unacceptable and they would have to find another way. They stagger out of the woods and manage to get back home a half mile away. They both pass out and fall asleep. When they wake they come to the reality that it wasn't all a dream. They come to the conclusion that they would commit suicide. The decision was made on what to do but now they had to decide on how to do it. They knew that they couldn't drink themselves to death they were trying to do that for years and that obviously wasn't working. One said how about hanging ourselves but his buddy said no. He said that might hurt and he didn't want pain. Finally one says let's take a shotgun and blow our own heads off. It will happen so quickly that we won't feel it. Good idea the other man says and they decide that the very next day would be the day. The following day they get two bottles of wine and some beer. They borrow a shotgun and a rifle from a friend. They say they want to go target practicing and the friend gives them the guns. They go to the area by the pond and start drinking. A couple of hours pass and they are both quit intoxicated. One of them gets up and said it's time. His friend said ok. They walk over by the pond. One man takes the shotgun, loads it and puts it in his mouth. As hard as he could he tried to pull the trigger as his friend stands by waiting his turn and cheers him on. He makes several attempts and finally said to his friend I just can't bring myself to killing myself. His friend said go ahead I'm waiting to go next. He said I can't you have to help me. His friend agrees and says go stand over there by that tree. The man does. His friend stands about 10 feet away, raises the shotgun, points it at his friend's chest and pulls the trigger. It does the job but as you can imagine it made a mess. He lowers the gun, looks at his friend and is devastated. He thinks that maybe this AIDS thing really isn't that bad. He decides not to kill himself. He now has another problem the body. He panics and then thinks I'll just bury him here. He likes it here and nobody ever comes by here anyway. He digs a hole and rolls his friend in. He covers him up, finishes the beer and throws the shot gun and rifle into the pond. He leaves and goes home. There is only one thing he overlooks, the hole wasn't deep enough and his friends shoulder was above ground. It wouldn't have been too bad except his red plaid shirt looked out of place. We all can see that this is much too easy. For a place that nobody ever goes to a man walking his dog discovers the body a few hours later. He calls the police.

Crime scene arrives and observes the scene with the partially buried victim. We examine the scene and see a large piece of bark missing from a nearby tree. There are also what appears to be drag marks going from the tree to the grave site.

They also see scuff marks by the pond. We take photographs and make a video recording. A search is made and evidence is recovered. We have wine bottles, beer cans and cigarette butts. The evidence is collected. We start to exhume the victim from the grave.

I must break from the story to tell you that was the first grave most of us had ever dug. We didn't have much equipment except for two folding army shovels, an ice scraper and a coffee sifter. This is about as primitive as it gets. After this scene we went to a school on how to exhume bodies. I'll explain that in detail in another chapter.

We exhume the victim's body and find that he suffered a chest wound directly to his heart. We recovered 9 shot pellets and the wad at the autopsy. In his pants pockets we found his wallet and a pack of cigarettes. The cigarettes were the same brands as the butts were that we picked up earlier. We also called in police divers who searched the pond and recovered the shotgun and the rifle. All the evidence was taken to the crime lab. Detectives went to the address they found in the victim's wallet and spoke to his friend. They asked him what happened and he told them the whole story and said that he was glad they caught him and that he was sorry. The case went to trial and he was sentenced to 25 years in prison. The rest of the story is that after all that had gone on neither one the men had AIDS. Did he really want to do this?

Let's take this up one level. A father and son are in the garage at their home. The father is working on some items that need repair and is having a heart to heart with his son. It really was more than that. The father and son have had problems. The son is a young teen and does some of the things a young teen boy would do. His school work could be better, he has tendencies to answer his mom back and forgets to do things like take the garbage out. The boy's father is a strict man that believes you do what you're told to do when you are told to do it. You don't answer your mother back, do all you school work right and don't forget your chores. He is always dissatisfied with the boy and what he does or doesn't do. On this day he grounds the young man and has the boy in the garage and is reprimanding him over and over. The boy sits and listens and sits and listens. Eventually it gets so repetitive that the boy tunes his father out. His father is enraged by this and slaps the boy. The boy stands up and says don't touch me again and picks up a knife that's on the work bench. His father jumps to his feet, stands in front of the boy and says go ahead kill me. You want to kill me? Go ahead. Listen to me he says kill me. The boy takes the knife and stabs his father once in the chest. The man falls to the ground. The boy runs in the house and dials the police and tells his mother what just happened. The police arrive and the father is taken away by ambulance. He dies hours later. The young boy can't believe what he did. He said dad kept saying do it, I said do it! The boy was charged with manslaughter and was given a 5 years sentence. Do you really want to do this? The next two cases that I am going to discuss have national notoriety. Both case changed people's lives. One case changed fundraising in schools and other organizations. In this case we have a young man in school. The school is having a fund rising whereby the students are asked to sell candy for a designated function within the school. The young man is enthusiastic about selling the candy and his goal is to sell more candy than the rest of the children in his class and win the prize. It started out as a bright sunny day when he started out into the neighborhood to get candy orders. It was an upscale well to do neighborhood. He left the house around 11 am. His mother assumed that at most he would be gone a couple of hours and then return home. A couple of hours turned into several and by the time it started getting dark he still wasn't home. She was concerned and called the police. The police came and took a missing persons report. They then started a search around the neighborhood. The boy's father and neighbors were out looking for him. It went well into the night and the searches didn't find anything but the search continued. The search went on into the next day and the next night. By this time hundreds of police, firefighters and local people were looking for him. The state police and FBI became involved in the search with high tech search equipment. Blood hounds, helicopter with infrared sensors and every available resource were being used. On the third day the boy's body was found in a shallow creek in the neighborhood. His body was stuffed into a suitcase. He had been strangled.

The crime scene unit was called in and we began processing the area. Photographs and a video recording were taken. A crime scene sketch was also made. The investigation went into the next day. We happen to notice that across the street from the place where the victim was found another boy was observing everything that we did. He watched us all day. Finally a car pulled into his driveway and he was about to get into it. Just before he did two detectives stopped him and asked him what he was doing and where he was going. A woman exited the car and said that she was his mother. The detectives told her that they would like to ask her son some questions. She resisted at first but then consented. They took the boy who was 16 years old and his mother to headquarters to question the boy. About four hours later we received a call that the boy had confessed to his mother about killing the boy, placing him in the suitcase and taking him across the street and leaving him in the creek. The crime now expanded to the 16 year olds residence. Search warrants were obtained and we moved our investigation to the residence. We concentrated our investigation to the 16 year olds room. In the room we found the victim's candy order form. A Polaroid photograph was found in the room. It was a photograph of the victim lying dead in the suitcase with a lamp cord around his neck. The 16 year old boy was taken into custody and charged with homicide.

The next problem was whether to pursue the suspect in trial as an adult or as juvenile? The difference being that if tried as adult he could be sentence to 30 years but if sentenced as a juvenile he could only sentenced to a maximum of 5 years. The judge ruled that he would stand trial as an adult. The trial was never needed the 16 year old pled guilty and received a 30 year sentence for homicide. Did you really want to do this?

Because of this case children no longer go door to door selling candy or anything else. The order forms are sent home and fund raising sales are done under the supervision of the student's parents.

This next case is another of national news. It's about noon and our victim is in between classes that she is attending. She is a school teacher and is furthering her education. She is married and has a son. She stops off in a shopping center to get some lunch and goes into a local pizza restaurant and gets some lunch. She finishes her lunch and goes to the parking lot to get into her car. As she does she is approached by a young male. He forces her into the car and gets in with her. He has a knife. He is driving. He drives the car south into the next town and turns off on to a dirt road. They drive about a quarter of a mile where the road turns on to another dirt road in the woods. This dirt road leads to a clearing where it appears to be a dumping ground. At the time they first left the parking lot where the victim had her lunch the victim managed to turn on a pocket tape recorder she had in her pocket. While they were driving she engaged the young man in conversation and had been recording it as they spoke. She asked him why he was doing this and he said that it was his birthday and he wanted her car. She had a Toyota Camry. He pulled the car over when they reached the clearing and shut the motor off. The victim was telling him that he could have the car and that she wouldn't say anything if he let her go. He said that he couldn't do that. He was going to have to kill her. She pled with him telling him that she had a little boy and even showed him his picture which she had in her bag of study materials. She handed him the picture, he took it, looked at it and handed it back to her. She put it back into the book and then put the book back into the bag. During this time the tape in her pocket tape recorder ran out. With the tape recorder still in her coat pocket she managed to take the tape out of the recorder, turn it over and put it back into the recorder and put the recorder back on. They talked for a while all the time she was pleading for her life. It was to no avail he bound her body and strangled her. He dumped her body on the side of the road in the trash pile and also emptied out the contents of the car and left it there as well. He then left her in the woods and went home taking the car with him.

The car was located in an apartment complex about midway between the spot where the victim was abducted and where he left her body. Her body was discovered in the woods about the same time as her car was found. She was found by a search party. When her car was found people in the parking lot told police whose car it was. The suspect told everyone that he got it for his birthday. The suspect was arrested and the car was impounded. The suspect said that his brother stole the car and gave it to him for his birthday. The bother denied that story and his mother confirmed that the brother was with her for the last couple of days. The vehicle was taken to the crime lab for processing.

A crime scene investigation was started in the woods. The evidence from the victim's car was collected and the victim's body was taken from the scene and sent to the morgue. A crime scene sketch was made along with the taking of photographs and video recording. The evidence was processed at the crime lab when we returned. On the picture of the victim's son that she had shown the actor we recovered two fingerprints. One was hers and one was the actors. These would later be important at the time of trial. The other piece of important evidence that would help at the trial was the tape recording. Prior to her death she had managed to get it from her pocket and put it in the same bag that we found the picture in.

At the trial the tape was played for the jury. The fingerprint expert proved that the two fingerprints on the photographs were one of hers and one of his. This was the same photographed that was mentioned on the tape when the victim was pleading for her life. The defendant denied killing the victim and still said that it was his brother. When asked about how his fingerprint got on the photograph he said that he helped his brother unload the car in the woods and that is probably how his fingerprint got on the photograph. The prosecutor asked the defendant if the photograph was in a book that was inside a lined pad which was inside another folder which was inside the bag how did his fingerprint get through all of those things onto the photograph. He said I guess I must have touched it somehow. The prosecutor asked do you really think that is possible. He said it's possible. Unfortunately the jury didn't agree with him. He was convicted of homicide and carjacking. He received a 30 year to life sentence for homicide and 20 years for the carjacking to be run consecutively. He wouldn't be eligible for parole for 40 years. Happy birthday! Did you really want to do this?

CHAPTER TEN

Digging Up Bones

In this section we will explore the underground crime scenes. One of the more difficult things to do as a crime scene investigator is to unearth a grave site. I became a specialist in this area along with another long time detective friend of mine. We found there was a desperate need for law enforcement to learn the proper techniques for unearthing victims from the ground. We actually started training law enforcement personal from all over the United States and some foreign countries as well. Federal law enforcement agencies used our techniques in places like Somalia, Kosovo and Iraq. You wouldn't think that there would actually be training for these things but there is. The University of Tennessee has an area where human and animal corpses are buried in different manners so as to study decomposition rates. They invite law enforcement personal to attend seminars at the farm to learn about decomposition. Law enforcement officers attend archeological classes to learn about excavation techniques. My partners and I attended both. We then developed a training class to instruct law enforcement personal in the proper method to excavate victims. Prior to this training we were doing things wrong. We were using backhoes and heavy equipment. Remember the case with the two alcoholics who thought they had Aids, we used a coffee sifter, ice scraper and army trenching shovel. We talked earlier about trace evidence and these antiquated methods lost a lot of evidence that may have solved cases. The new methods are really some of the oldest. When a body is exhumed these days it's done in the same manner that an Egyptian tomb is excavated. We grid off an area and use small hand shovels to dig along with dental picks, tongue depressors and paint brushes. The soil is removed in buckets and pails. It's then sifted through screens that get finer and finer. Instead of it taking a couple of hours it can take a couple of days or longer. Where speed was your necessity it is now your enemy. Sure everyone wants to get going looking for suspects but taking your time can actually speed things up and crucial evidence isn't missed as easily. There are some new technologies used as well today. One is a piece of equipment that was developed to find underground pipes but it works just as well when looking for bodies. It's called ground penetrating radar. It works the same way regular radar works using radio waves. It really doesn't show you a picture but it does show the differences in soil densities. When someone digs a trench or a hole in the ground they displace the soil which has been sitting undisturbed until you moved it. Its compaction is gone. I know you're thinking what if the person who dug the hole packs the dirt down when the hole is filled in? The problem with this thought is that it is impossible to replace the soil in exactly the same place it came from. Re placement of the soil changes the soils density. The ground penetrating radar shows these changes. Density of soil differs from density of human flesh or bone or concrete pipe.

The case studies here will be different not only in the stories behind them but in the methods of recovery used.

This first case starts out with a funny twist. Two men were in the woods collecting aluminum cans along a dirt road that people have dumped trash. They come upon a clearing that visibly has some cans lying around in it. They separate and start collecting their cans when one of them comes upon what appears to be a decomposing body. He calls his friend over and they decide to call the police. They exit the woods onto the roadway and cross the street to a concrete plant where they ask to use the telephone. They call the police who arrive and they tell them what they found. The police tell them to take them to the body but they refuse. They tell the police to take them to the recycling center so they can redeem their cans first. The police ask why and one of them says that if we don't redeem the cans first you'll take them from us for evidence and we'll lose money. After a while the police finally give in and take the two men to the recycling center to redeem their cans. The two men then take the police to the wooded area across from the concrete plant to the clearing alongside the dirt road.

The police view the body in the clearing and see that it is the body of a woman. The body is partially decomposed and partially mummified. The body is fully clothed and lying on the surface of the ground. Grass is growing around the body which is about 8 inches high. Also in the area there is scattered trash and junk. The clearing area is approximately 100 feet by 100 feet. The responding officers call the crime scene unit. The crime scene unit arrives and examines the area. In addition to the items seen by the responding officers the crime scene unit locates a pocketbook and the victim's shoes. The entire area has about 8 inches of a thin grass covering over it. An examination of the body didn't exhibit any signs of trauma. The victim's upper body was decomposed to a point to where there wasn't very much tissue remaining. There was still some hair remaining on the skull. The lower portion of the body was clothed and mummified probably due to the extreme heat of the recent weeks and the blue jeans that covered the lower half of the body. Mummification is a process that under the proper conditions causes the body tissues to dry out rather than decompose. The dry tissue will then adhere to the bones in their dry state and take on harden texture. The mummification process is somewhat of a rarity and not seen that often.

In most cases of this nature where a body is found on the surface all of the bones are first photographed and carefully sketched in their location. They are then collected and examined by the medical examiner. The medical examiner carefully checks each bone for any signs of trauma such a break or nicks and other abnormalities. The bones are then reconstructed back to their anatomical location. In this particular case we used a new procedure. Instead of collecting each bone separately we chose to remove the victim's entire body in its existing state. In order to accomplish this we needed to excavate the soil under the victim and keep the soil in place. We did this by digging a trench around the body and then using machetes cut the soil about 4 inches under the body. A piece of plywood was then slid under the cut soil and the entire body was lifted to from the ground. This procedure allows the actual crime scene to be presented to the medical examiner. In some cases this can be very helpful to the medical examiner when trying to determine the cause of death. This is called the plateau method because the body is raised from the ground on the plateau created by the excavation. At the autopsy the medical examiner could not make a determination as to the cause of death. These results would be pending the outcome of a toxicology report. Toxicology is a chemical test used to determine if poisons or other toxins were introduced to the body. Due to the lack of evidence to determine the cause of death the area was searched for evidence which may have led to the victim's death. The victim was identified by identification found in the pocketbook recovered at the scene. She had also been reported as a missing person. During the investigation we learned where she lived and who she lived with. Her boyfriend was questioned but said he hadn't seen her in 6 months since she had gone missing. No other evidence was recovered at the search however the toxicology report results came back as showing high levels of cocaine in the victim's system. In addition a soil sample take from the ground from under the victim's body also was positive for cocaine. The medical examiner then could make a determination as to the cause of death, a drug overdose. The victim's boyfriend was questioned again and this time he told the detectives that they had in fact been using cocaine. He said that she all of a sudden collapsed and died. He said that he was afraid that someone might have thought that he killed her so he took her body to the woods by the concrete plant and left her in the woods. He knew the area because he drove a concrete truck for a living and had been in the woods in that area before. As a result the boyfriend was charged with illegal disposition of a body, fined and released.

Our next case begins with a man and his wife walking on a path in the woods to get to a lake that they fish in when they have time. On this particular day they were walking down the path as they have done in the past. In the path was a pile of what appeared to be roofing materials. They actually made several trips back and forth along the path that day. On one trip they saw a strange object coming out from under some roofing shingles. He moved the shingles and saw that it was a body. He went to the roadside and called the police. When the police arrived he took them to the body which was about a quarter of a mile from the road. The officer examined the scene and called the crime scene unit. The crime scene unit arrived and examined the scene. The body was under a pile of roofing shingles about 2 feet high and then a sheet of plywood was on top of the shingles. The entire area was over grown with thick brush except for the narrow path leading to the lake. The first order of business was to cut down the brush. A team of officers armed with branch loppers, pruning shears and small knives then proceeded to remove the brush. The branches were cut down and removed one by one until an area in a 25 foot circle was cleared. Everything was removed down to ground level including the grass. No additional evidence was found during the search. The roofing materials were removed from the body one at a time and examined for any trace evidence. After the roofing materials were removed the detectives observed the victim. The victim's body was completely skeletonized. The only part of the body that contained any tissue was the heel of the victim's left foot. That was the only portion of the victim that was visible from under the shingles. There appeared to be a hole in the victim's chest. It was about one and a half inches in diameter. The bones were photographed, sketched and collected into evidence in the same manner as in the previously recovered body using the plateau method. There was no way to identify the victim at this point other than by the bones which could only tell us at this point that the victim was female. An expanded search was made of the area and the victim's pocketbook and clothing were found. It turned out that she was reported missing 2 months prior. The amazing thing about this is that the body completely skeletonized in two months. The happened because of the atmospheric conditions present during that time. It was extremely hot with very low humidity. In addition the body was buried under the roofing shingles which retained the heat of the day and lying on the damp ground near the lake causing the decomposition process to accelerate. Under normal conditions this process should have taken close to a year.

The ensuing investigation by detectives led the detectives to the rooming house in which the victim lived. While asking questions at the rooming house they found out the victim was having problems with another one of the rooming house residents. She had several clashes with him in the past. He wasn't there when the detectives looked for him and had apparently left town a couple of days before. It was also learned during the investigation that the medical examiner said that the cause of death was due to a shotgun blast to the chest. Shot shell pellets were found in the soil under the victim which had sunk to the ground during the decomposition of the body. The suspect was eventually located, arrested and charged with homicide.

This next case was one of the most difficult from an emotional stand point. Our victim is a 14 year old high school student. She has a boyfriend which is nothing unusual for a girl her age. They also have relationship problems which is also not unusual for a girl her age. She also has problems at home with her father and stepmother. It even erupted to a domestic problem at one time. Other problems existed in and around her life. Her father had a drug problem and she had been arrested once as a juvenile. On this day in question she had an argument with her boyfriend and decided to walk home. It was a long walk but she headed out anyway. While walking home she met one of her father's friends. He was talking with another man by his car. She asked him if they would give her a ride home and they said yes. On the way her father's friend dropped off the man he was talking to and then they proceeded on. That was the last time she was seen. When she didn't return home that evening her father became concerned and called her mother to see if she had gone there, when she said no they called police and filed a missing persons report. The police investigated the case for several days without any luck. They finally got a break when the fathers drug dealer made an anonymous call that the girl was last seen with two men one of which was her father's friend. It seemed that the man was owed drug money by some of the men and this was his way to get back at them. The police knew the man who was dropped off and went to his home to get him. He was home and agreed to answer questions. During the questioning he told the detectives the name of the man who was driving the car. They questioned the man but didn't get very much information and released him. They felt that their best option was to get more information from the first man that they questioned. They went back to his house but he wasn't home. They decided to wait for him. They waited all night but he didn't come home. It was about 5:45 in the morning and they were just getting ready to leave. At that moment they saw the second man they questioned walking down the street with a gas can. He walked up to the second man's house and started splashing gas on it. They arrested him on the spot for attempted arson. He was held and questioned again. When he was arrested his name was run for warrants. It just so happened that a few days before an officer in an adjoining town had stopped him coming out of the woods in her town. The officer said she was on normal patrol in the area where woods and power lines separated the two towns. It was a misty rainy day and as she turned the corner she saw a car stopped on the side of the road, near the woods. The car was running, the lights and wipers were on and the driver's door was open. She didn't see anybody in the car so she turned around to investigate. As she pulled up behind the car she observed a man walking out of the woods. She asked him if this was his car and he said it was. She asked if anything was wrong and he responded that his dog got loose and he was looking for him. She checked his documents and inquired as to why he was looking for the dog in this town and not his. He said that he lived in the next town on the other side of the woods and that the dog had run off into the woods. She filled a field inquiry card and went back to her normal duties.

Detectives suspected fowl play and decided to search the woods and power lines area. The area was very large so additional help was needed. They got help from local volunteer fire companies. About 200 searchers entered the woods and power line fields and walked shoulder to shoulder twice but come up empty. The search was temporarily called off. The next morning while a new search was being formulated an off duty corrections officer was training his cadaver dog. He was having the dog search the area of the power lines where the search had been conducted the day before. The dog seemed interested in a particular area so they called for the crime scene unit. We responded and determined that the soils in that area were disturbed. We did this with two 48 inch metal probs. If the soil was undisturbed the ground would be hard. If it was recently dug the ground would be loose and soft and it was. We continued probing to define just how large the area was. After finding the edges of the trench we divided the area into grids and began to excavate the ground. At a depth of 16 inches from the surface we uncovered what turned out to be an arm. On the arm was a bracelet. The bracelet was removed and taken to the missing girl's parents and they confirmed that in fact the bracelet belonged to their daughter. A short time later as the excavation continued we uncovered a necklace around the victim's neck which bore her name. During the dig the dirt being removed from the grave was sifted for trace evidence of which very little was found. The victim's body was completely uncovered and she was removed from the grave and pronounced dead by the medical examiner. She was then transported to the morgue for an autopsy. The area under the body was thoroughly examined to see if the actor left behind any additional evidence such as a footwear impression. Think about it he had to stand in the hole to dig it out. After the examination soil samples were taken for analysis. The autopsy told us that she was dead prior to being buried but that she had been suffocated. She was not sexually assaulted but that she had some minor trauma to the nose area.

During the investigation the suspect's car was taken into evidence and processed. During the processing a blood drop was recovered from the headliner on the passenger side of the vehicle. The evidence was enough to convict the actor. He was sentenced to 30 years to life with no eligibility for parole for 30 years.

One other case involving burials comes to mind. We had a serial killer in our area that is well known. He murdered several people before being caught. He would always bury his victims after he killed them. When he buried the first victim she was 6 feet underground. Twenty three victims later the last victim found was partially exposed. We know because he has stated it many times that we still haven't found all of his victims.

CHAPTER ELEVEN

All Rise

In this section I will try to explain some of the court proceedings that forensic detectives and investigators testify to. I will try to explain just who does what. The best place to start is at the top the Judge. The Judge is a public officer authorized to hear and decide cases in a court of law. He hears cases and oversees the proceedings. He insures that the trial or hearings are held in accordance to the law. There are many rules and procedures that must be followed and it is the Judge's job to see that these things are followed and to maintain order within the court.

There are also other people in the courtroom who have specific jobs to do. There is a court clerk, who is an officer of the court whose responsibilities include maintaining the records of the court. Another duty is to administer oaths to witnesses, jurors, and grand jurors. Traditionally, the clerk also was the custodian of the court's seal, which is used to authenticate copies of the court's orders, judgments and other records. The clerk usually sits close to the Judge. Another person you will see in a courtroom is the official court recorder. The court reporter is a person whose occupation is to transcribe spoken or recorded speech into written form, typically using machine shorthand or a voice silencer and digital recorder to produce official transcripts of court hearings, depositions and other official proceedings.

There are others in the courtroom whose job it is to maintain security. These people may be Sheriff's Officers, Court Officers, Police Officers, Bailiffs or Matrons. These officers work at the discretion of the judge. They may remove or bring prisoners to the court. Escort witnesses to and from the witness stand. They transfer papers from litigants to the judge. They call the court to order and escort the judge into and out of the courtroom. They assist jurors and other persons within the courtroom. They maintain quiet during the proceedings.

Besides the people who work in the courtroom there are people who participate in the proceedings. First of all and one of the most important is the jury. The jury is the people who will decide which side is right or wrong. Their job is to listen to all the testimony from all the witnesses, attorneys, plaintiffs, defendants and instructions from the Judge. At the conclusion of the testimony phase of the trial the jury takes all the evidence and exhibits into the jury room and deliberate the facts to reach a verdict. In smaller civil matters and in family court matters there isn't a jury. These decisions are made by the Judge.

Next we have the witnesses. It is their job to present testimony to the court. The testimony they provide may be for the prosecution or the defense. Witnesses can be law enforcement personal, citizens or experts in the field of knowledge that is at question. You may ask what the difference is. When a witness is certified by the court as an expert a witness it gives their testimony an option not given to regular witnesses. A regular witness is only allowed to testify to personal knowledge and facts. They can't form an opinion. An expert witness is an expert in a particular field of knowledge like hand writing analysis. A regular witness is held to a yes that is his signature. He can also say that is not his signature. An expert witness can say that after my examination and analysis it is in **my opinion,** his signature. Through the experts training and experience the expert is allowed to form an opinion. Their work is usually backed up by reports of analysis and findings and is clearly documented. Experts may be called upon to testify against other experts and the jury is left to decide which one is right.

The next two participants in the courtroom are the plaintiffs and the defendants. The plaintiff is the person presenting the case to the court. In a criminal case that could be the State, County or Local Municipality. In other proceeding it could be a neighbor against another neighbor or a landlord against a tenant. It could be a wife against a husband. The defendant on the other hand is usually the accused. The defendant is the person who has to answer the charge against him. That brings us to the attorneys. These are people with degrees in law that assist the plaintiff or defendants present their case in court. These things are usually preceded with forms and papers that the attorneys file with the court. In a criminal case the attorney presenting the plaintiffs side is usually called the Prosecutor or the District Attorney. They rarely have a person as a plaintiff. They represent the "people" of the State, County or Local Municipality. They present the facts of the case to the jury. The attorney for the defendant is usually called the Defense. It is their job to present a defense of the charges to the jury. They almost always have a person next to them usually the defendant.

Forensic witnesses bring evidence to the court that prove or disprove the facts. This can be in the form of reports or documents. They present physical, visible and verbal testimony to the proceedings. This can come in the form of charts, graphs, photographs and video. They can get elaborate and present exhibits like reconstructed models, visual presentations like power point. Juries understand things better when they can see what the witness is explaining as well as listening to their testimony. I can sit and explain to you how a fingerprint comparison is made but if I put it up on a large screen in front of you and take you through an example of how it's done you will get a better understanding of it. To see it being done while it is being explained to you will help you have a better understanding of how it is done.

Trials have an order they follow. First a charge is filed. Then a decision is made on whether or not there are sufficient grounds to bring the matter to trial. Once it is decided to go forward motions are filed to go to trial. There is then what they call a pretrial hearing before the Judge. The Judge will decide if he/she feels there is enough to go forward with a trial. If he does a trial date is set. There are meetings between the Judge and the attorneys, meetings between the defense attorney and the defendant, meeting between the witnesses and the prosecution. Jury selection is made. This is where the attorneys and the judge pick a jury for a trial. They call potential jurors to the stand and the attorneys ask them questions to qualify them for the trial. The attorneys are allowed a given amount of challenges to the juror. They can keep or dismiss the juror if they wish without question. Some questions they ask is your employment, are you related to the litigants, do you know anyone on the witness list etc. Once a jury is selected the trial will start. In court the first thing that happens are some instruction from the Judge. The attorneys then are allowed opening statements. This is their chance to briefly lay out their case. Usually the prosecution goes first then the defense will speak. The prosecution will then begin to call his witnesses and present his case to the court. As he calls his witnesses and questions them, the defense will then have a chance to question the witness. This is called cross examination. When he is done the prosecution will rest. It then becomes the defenses chance to present his defense. He too will call witnesses and question them and the prosecution will have a chance to cross examine the witness. When he is complete he will say the defense rest. The testimony is now done. The Judge will then charge the jury. That means he will instruct the jury as to the law and how it applies to the case. The jury will then retire to the jury room where they will deliberate the case. All the exhibits and evidence will go with the jury. The jury may also request to have testimony of the witnesses read back to them if necessary. Once they make a decision of which there are three, Guilty, Not Guilty or what's called a Hung Jury. Hung Jury means that a decision could not be reached. Guilty or Not guilty verdicts must be unanimous. If the jury cannot reach a verdict the Judge declares a mistrial and the case are retried with a new jury. The procedure starts all over again. If they return a guilty or not guilty verdict the Judge will call the court back in session and verdict is read. If the verdict is not guilty the defendant is released. If the verdict is guilty the Judge may or may not set bail until sentencing. If he doesn't the defendant is remanded to jail until sentencing. He will then set a sentencing date. On the sentencing day the defendant is sentenced and the case is closed.

CHAPTER TWELVE

The Scene Behind The Scene

This section will take you inside the crime laboratory. I will break it down by sections and explain what each section does and give an overview of what type of equipment is used and how it is used and how the results are received. First of all a Crime Lab is a scientific laboratory using primarily forensic science for the purpose of examining evidence from crime scenes. Next we ask ourselves what is Forensic Science. Forensic science is the application of a broad spectrum of sciences to answer question of interest to the legal system. It is where evidence that can't be processed in the field is processed.

The best place to start is at the front door. As we said the crime lab is where evidence is processed. The evidence comes from crime detectives or it can be brought to the lab from outside agencies that don't have their own crime labs. When the evidence is brought into the lab it is logged in. This is called the intake section. That means that a paper trail is started so the evidence can be followed through every process. It keeps a record of all the persons who processed it. Once it is logged in a decision is made as to what type of processing is required and what result the submitter is seeking. For instance, if fingerprints are what the submitter is looking for the item is taken to fingerprint processing. In that section the item will be dusted, fumed or treated with chemicals to produce a positive or negative result. From intake the evidence is taken to its required section and the process has begun. The sections we will be covering are Latent Fingerprint, Fingerprint Comparison, Ballistic, Video Analysis, Photographic Services, Trace Evidence, Chemical and Biological Analysis, Questioned Documents, Fractured Edge and Arson Analysis. There are others but these are the most common. I'll go through them one by one in no particular order.

The first section is the Chemical and Biological Analysis. This is your chemical laboratory. It looks like your chemistry laboratory in high school or college. In this laboratory substances are analyzed to determine if they are CDS, controlled dangerous substances, drugs. This process is accomplished in a piece of equipment called a GC Mass Spectrometer. This machine takes the substance, heats it up to produce a gas and then breaks the gas down into its chemical elements. Depending on the quantity of the elements and the combinations of the elements it can determine what the substance is. The machine is operated by a computer and the computer has an internal library that it compares the results to determine the substance. In addition to drug testing the machine analyzes other substances to determine what they are such as an accelerant in an Arson examination. Also in this laboratory in the Biological section is where the DNA testing is done. DNA testing is the examining of biological fluids to determine their origins. It's a little more involved than that. The sample must first be extracted, or collected and then put in a machine that amplifies the sample. That means it takes a small sample and makes it larger. As I said there is more to it than that but that's about as simple as I can make it. The amplified samples are compared to other samples and see if they match. This is an exacting science in the field of identification as like in fingerprints with one exception. In the case of identical twins, meaning boy—boy or girl—girl, the identification codes are too close to distinguish the difference. In in addition to analyzing substances the weights of the substances are determined. You ask why the weight of the substance so important, well when charging persons with drug offenses the degree of the crime depends on the weight of the substance. That could be the difference between a possession charge or a distribution charge or a trafficking charge. In the biological section clothing and body fluid samples are tested for DNA in sexual assault cases as well. DNA is also used by the courts in paternity cases to determine who a child's father is.

Next we have the ballistics section. This is where all firearms, ammunition, shell casings and projectiles are examined and or compared. When a fire arm is brought into the ballistics laboratory it almost always test fired. When it is test fired the projectile and shell casing are collected, photographed and saved into evidence. A library of them is saved so they can be compared to other projectiles that are brought into the lab. Sometimes a projectile or casing from one shooting can tie into another shooting. Solve one crime and maybe solve another. These items are examined and compared under a comparison microscope. A comparison microscope is similar to a standard microscope with one exception it has two viewing stations that connect to one eyepiece that allows two items to be looked at the same time. The ballistics laboratory also restores filed off or defaced serial numbers on weapons. In most cases firearms that are in the ballistics lab they are also sent to the latent fingerprint lab to be examined for fingerprints.

For the most part Arson evidence is tested in the chemical laboratory. Fluid samples and collected materials evidence extractions are analyzed in GC Mass Spectrometer. Other pieces of evidence like a gas can or a bottle are sent to the latent fingerprint laboratory to see if fingerprints can be developed.

Trace Evidence is small particles such as hairs and fibers. These items are usually examined under a microscope. A comparison microscope comes in handy here as well. This examination is quit involved and requires a lot of training and a lot of samples in a database for comparison. Don't even think about the hairs but can you imagine how many fiber types there are? Hairs can determine race and identity as well as human and animal.

Fractured Edge examinations are usually forensic jigsaw puzzles. Fracture edge is exactly what it says. In the case of a hit and run motor vehicle accident lens covers break. The pieces of lens left on a roadway are brought to the lab. They are compared to the lens pieces of a suspect vehicle by putting the pieces together the same way you put a jigsaw puzzle together. The same system is used with torn paper, broken windows and sometimes even body parts.

Questioned Documents covers a couple of things. It covers forgery, hand writing analysis and things like typewriter marks. Forged papers sometimes contain water marks or even fibers in the paper. Hand writing analysis examiners look at writings and determine if the writing are from the suggested person or someone else. They examine the flow of the writings, the slant of the letters and the actual letter formation and line spacing.

Photographic services are the reproduction of photographs, the enlarging of photographs, the developing film and photographic mediums. The enhancement of photographs and assemble of photographs to create a larger view. They also specialize in the taking of photographs which require special equipment and special conditions. Working hand and hand with photographic services is the video enhancement section. They take videos from surveillance cameras and enhance them and collect still photographs from videos. Many an actor was caught by video enhancement. The most frequent would be bank robbers. Banks have many cameras that not only watch the patrons but the employees as well.

This brings us to the latent fingerprint laboratory. It is their job to take the submitted evidence and process it for fingerprints. It is probably is one of the most used services of the crime laboratory. The latent fingerprint laboratory uses dusting powders, chemical, enhanced lighting, fuming chambers, humidity chambers and lasers to accomplish their task. The processes are so varied and different that entire books have been written on the subject. Every piece of evidence presents its own set of problems when it comes to developing fingerprints. It depends on the item, the texture of the item and size of the item. Taking those issues into consideration determines what process is required to get the results. It may entail using chemicals or dusting powders. At times the detectives or technicians have to go to extremes to reach their goal. At other times the process works relatively easily.

That brings us to the fingerprint comparison section. These people must physically look at the known print and the unknown fingerprint to see if they match. I know you see computers on television selecting fingerprints from a database and getting a match. That's true however even after the computer makes a match a human must compare the two fingerprints. Computers are machines and make errors. That's not to say humans don't make errors they do that's why a fingerprint must be examined by more than one examiner and those examiners must agree on the result. If one says it is and the other says it isn't it's considered to be a negative. The is no middle of the road when it comes to fingerprints it's either positive or negative.

We have now gone through the crime laboratory and processed our evidence. Now what? The completed evidence is now placed into storage and either returned to the agency that submitted it or it is held for trial. The reports are issued and the work is done . . . for now.

I would like to say the persons who process crime scenes and process the evidence have many hours of training. They attend many schools in their area of expertise. The training is ongoing because technology changes all the time and these people must keep up with the latest in technology.